IT'S A SET UP

GRAND MARQUEE MANTICORES
BOOK 0.5

STEF C.R.

COPYRIGHT

It's a Set Up

Copyright © 2025 Stef C. R.

All rights reserved. No part of this book may be reproduced in any form except for the purpose of brief reviews or citations without the written permission of the author.

This is a work of fiction in which all events and characters in this book are completely imaginary. Any resemblance to actual people is entirely coincidental.

Cover designed by Lorissa Padilla.
Book edited by Erin King.

ALSO BY STEF C.R.

Grand Marquee Manticores
The Love Penalty (#1)
Bar Down (#2)

DEDICATION

If you consider teasing to be a love language, this one's for you!

AUTHOR'S NOTE

While this book is a funny and cute sports romance, there are mentions of sibling death (off page), explicit sex scenes, and manipulation (by a role model). If you are not comfortable with any of the above, please skip this novella or contact me at stef@stefwritesstories.com with any questions or concerns!

ONE

The clock on the wall shows fifteen minutes past nine as I rapidly tap my foot against the tiled floor, my light pink sneakers squeaking against it with each movement as I finish my peanut butter granola bar. My alarm didn't go off this morning and I didn't have time to take a shower after my run. I figured I could take one at the arena and sneak a coffee in as well, but the gates of hell must be open because every possible living human in Grand Marquee decided The Cap was the café they needed to come to today.

This has been my go-to spot since I first moved here from Hawaii five years ago for college. My parents were a little crushed when I chose to move all the way to Michigan, but the volleyball scholarship helped a lot. Ultimately, they wanted me to follow my dream of playing in a professional league even if I had to travel an ocean away to reach it. The only downside is that I haven't been able to visit them since.

I glance around the bright café, admiring the cream-colored walls and all the plants on display—ferns, cacti, and spider plants. It's funny how I've come here every day for years and barely noticed how cool this place is. I often had my nose buried in a textbook while sitting at one of these tables, and since I graduated a little over six months ago, I've been so busy training that my coffee has only been taken to go.

Speaking of coffee...

If I don't get my drink soon, I'm going to be late to my meeting with Coach Jackson. As a newly minted women's professional volleyball team, we have a lot of work to do when it comes to training and practice. Our season doesn't even start for another three months, yet we're already hitting the ground running.

Today is an important milestone. We're meeting with both the captain and the coach of the Manticores hockey team to discuss schedules and facilities since we'll be sharing the arena.

"I've got an Americano ready!" the barista yells out over the crowd of people, and my sneaker squeaks again as I push my way through with a mumbled apology.

I'm blissfully close to my lord and savior, the Americano, when out of nowhere a giant paw grabs the small cup and brings it to a gaping face hole.

No, that's not a paw, it's the giant hand of a man who could probably crush me with his pinky alone. And the gaping face hole is a perfectly sculpted mouth. *Holy hell, where did he even come from?* He can't be less than 6'5", which is a whole foot taller than me. I'm sure I'll get a crick in my neck from looking up at him. But I can't stop.

The giant next to me takes a few more sips from my Americano and I just watch his pronounced Adam's apple bob with the movement. When he lowers the drink, I admire the way the light green T-shirt he's wearing hugs his torso and arms, which are covered in tattoos. Full sleeves of black ink in various shapes and sizes, with words and numbers interspersed throughout the designs that stop at his wrists.

The small cup changes hands and he looks down, noticing me for the first time. He has black hair that pokes out of his backwards hat and his matching black eyebrows lift as he considers me.

"Can I help you?" his deep and rich voice asks, and I think I might actually melt to the spot. I've seen my fair share of attractive people, especially growing up in Hawaii, where my friends and I would surf and spend most of our time playing beach volleyball, but there's something about this guy that makes me more nervous than usual. He's intimidating, but in a sexy way. Like he could throw me around in the bedroom and I'd probably beg for more.

"I—um, that's—" I stutter and point at his cup, but he doesn't look away from my face. *Is it hot in here?* My cheeks are on fire. *Does he think I'm having a stroke?*

I clear my throat and try again, "That's my drink."

The stranger's lips part and a small grin takes over his face. "Don't think so, sweetheart. I just ordered this."

My insides flutter at the way he calls me *sweetheart* but a small part of me is annoyed. I've been waiting here for fifteen minutes for my drink and he just ordered his?

"Do you not see the giant line? I ordered first and I've been waiting longer," I say, pointing to the drink and the crowded café around us.

His mossy green eyes lazily take in the room around him before they land on me again. "Fair enough." He leans in, bringing his gaze closer to mine and says, "How about you give me your number, and I'll have Drew here make you your coffee right now?"

I laugh at his offer, "They're not going to make you a coffee on the spot just because you asked."

"Hey Drew, I need another Americano as quickly as possible," he says, looking at the overwhelmed barista. I expect him to get yelled at or chewed out, but the blond guy just nods and says, "Right away, man."

I blink, mouth agape, because how the hell did he do that? I'm a regular here and not once has Drew remembered my order. Or my name, for that matter.

The stranger in front of me takes a pen out of his back pocket and hands it to me with a smirk that I should find smug but my brain unhelpfully interprets as sexy. I reluctantly take it and grab a napkin from the counter. In a burst of confidence, I turn back to him and place the napkin on his chest, looking coyly up at him a few times as I scribble down my phone number.

His chest puffs out the smallest bit and I tamp down my smile. Giving my number to a sexy guy is not what I expected on this busy day. I hand him the napkin with his pen, and he pockets them both. He leans in as he reaches behind me, and his proximity jumbles up my brain. It takes me longer than it should to realize he's presenting me with my coffee. "A deal's a deal, *sweetheart*."

"I have a name, you know," I say, my fingers wrapping around the small coffee cup. With one last glance at his green eyes, I step around him.

"You gonna tell me what it is?" he asks from behind me as I make my way to the door.

"Nah, I think you need to work a little harder for it," I say, giving him a smile over my shoulder, and swinging my hips as I walk away from him. Not only are these leggings great for running, but they also make my ass look amazing.

While the past few months have been stressful—learning to navigate my new position as captain of the Thunderbirds, going through gruesome personal training, and missing my family—for the first time in a while, I feel lighter and in control of the situation.

I smile all the way to the arena at the memory of the stranger's deep chuckle.

"CAP! HAVE YOU MET HIM YET?" Jonie, my teammate and one of my few close friends, says.

"Met who?" I ask, my dark brown eyebrows scrunched up in confusion. I don't hear her answer as my phone dings in the back of my pocket. I quickly take it out, thinking it's a message from my family, but no—it's a text from an unknown number.

> How many guesses do I get until you tell me your name?

My stomach flutters as I smile and shake my head, even though the tattooed stranger can't see me. I expected him to take a while to make a move, but he seems eager.

> Three.

> Only three? That's harsh, Ashley.

> Two left…

> Do I get any hints?

> No, I want to see what you come up with.

> You are one tough cookie, Alana.

> Wow, you are one impatient person.

> Makes sense, since you stole my Americano :)

> One left.

"Girl, who are you texting with that grin on your face?" Jonie says, reading over my shoulder.

"Mind your business," I tease, and hide the phone away from her view.

"You didn't answer me, have you met the Manticores captain yet? I hear he's panty-melting hot."

My nose scrunches and I snort. "Right, and he probably has some missing teeth too."

She mocks hurt and gasps, "Sacrilege! No, but seriously, Andrea said she saw him in person and he's hot as hell."

I doubt anyone could be as hot as my mystery guy from the café, but I let Jonie get it out of her system.

"You know the last thing we need is a distraction like that."

"Like what? Men?" she asks, cocking her head and twirling a dark red strand of hair through her fingers.

"Yes. Those. Dangerous, dangerous creatures," I mumble with a small smile, thinking about tattoos and muscular forearms.

"Mm-hmm. Tell me that again after you meet him," she says, ducking into the indoor gym and leaving me in the hallway.

MY SMILE VANISHES as soon as I approach Coach Jackson's office. His raised tone reaches my ears before I even turn the corner. With a deep breath, I throw the empty coffee cup in the nearest bin and make my way towards him.

"This schedule is unacceptable," he says hotly to his assistant. The poor kid has been his intern all summer and is barely hanging on by a thread. It can't possibly be fine for someone to get yelled at 24/7, and I'm surprised he hasn't quit yet. "Did you even listen to anything I said this morning?"

"Yes, sir, but that's out of my control, you'll have to take it up with the Manticores' coach."

"Great, so you're basically useless. Get out of my sight," Jackson tells his assistant, who rushes past me, cheeks red from anger and embarrassment. I feel bad for him, because I've been on the receiving end of those barbs myself. Jackson truly has a way to make people feel worthless.

I met Jackson on my first day of school, as he was my college volleyball coach. He's been by my side from the start, making sure I'm always at my best, making volleyball a priority. At first, I was so grateful for all the extra care and time he's put into training me—I still am—but ever since graduation, he's been extra hard. Not just on me, but on everybody on the team.

When he told me he was working with a new organization to start a professional women's volleyball team, I was thrilled. And when he proposed I take on the role of interim captain for our first season, I cried with joy and video-called my parents to bask in the great news. What I didn't realize was how fast everything was moving and that I wouldn't be able to go back home for the summer. Jackson insisted I stay here and train with him, get to understand the ins and outs of what it means to be on a professional team, and assist him in meetings.

I was torn between my guilt over not visiting home in

years and my guilt over leaving the team and missing out on training. Ultimately, I stayed, because I owe my coach everything for getting me this far in my career. I wouldn't be here without him.

I count to three before I walk up to Jackson, hoping he won't take his anger out on me. "Coach," I say with as much confidence as I can muster, trying not to let him see how much his mood affects me.

Jackson whips around and settles his cold, dark gaze on me, eyes assessing my outfit. "What the hell are you wearing? For fuck's sake, what if this meeting was more formal?"

I bite my tongue and look down as I mumble, "I hope you'd have told me if that was the case."

Jackson hears me anyway and glares at me. "Get your ass in that conference room."

I nod and walk down the hallway, making my way to the administrative offices and the conference room where our meeting is supposed to take place. I grimace at my sweaty clothes and hope that the Manticores' captain and coach don't actually care about my appearance, but Jackson's comment nags at me.

As I approach the room, I can hear parts of their conversation through the slightly open door. I'm getting ready to knock before pushing it all the way open, but what they're saying stops me in my tracks.

"This is a joke, Michael, why are we even giving in to any of their demands?" the first voice says in a deep tone.

"Play nice, Dionis, the last thing we need is a feud. Besides, we've shared the arena before. I know it's been a couple of years since, but we'll manage."

"It's not about the fact that we need to share the arena. It's the fact that it cuts into our gym and wellness time, and we're already a month into our season."

"I know, I know. We can negotiate some of these requests, don't get your panties all up in a twist," his coach says.

"What do they need three months before the season to train for? Do they suck that bad?" he snickers.

Okay, that's it. Before I realize what I'm doing, I'm pushing the door open all the way, not even flinching as it slams into the wall. "What the hell is your problem? Did you maybe take too many pucks to the head? Because this is not the way to start off this partnership."

"Partnership?" the captain says, turning on his heel and glaring down at me. And I'm pinned by *those eyes*. Those fucking gorgeous green eyes that I haven't been able to stop thinking about all morning.

"You," we say at the same time. His eyes widen while mine narrow, and I cross my arms over my chest, while he—the stranger who I now realize is Alex Dionis—puts his hands on his hips, the movement making him look bigger and more intimidating.

"You and your team of airheads waltzed in here and demanded we roll over and give you what you want," he says, shaking his head.

"We didn't do any of that. But you know what? We need to practice. Unlike your barbarian sport, we require finesse and teamwork," I say in a sweet voice, standing up straighter.

Alex laughs but his gaze narrows on me. "You're telling me about teamwork. Do you even know what hockey is?"

"Yes, I know what hockey is." I roll my eyes and drop my hands from my chest.

"What do you do? Hit a ball all day?" he taunts, green eyes glinting with mischief.

I already regret giving him my number. My hands are

balled into fists at my side and while I'm not a violent person, I would love nothing more than to show this guy what a spike is. *Maybe use his head as a volleyball.* For practice, of course.

His coach, Michael, takes a step closer to us and sighs. "This meeting was so you could get acquainted with one another and for us to go over the schedules, but maybe that needs to be rescheduled."

"Fine," Alex says in a hard tone.

"Great," I bite out and turn my back on Alex to leave the room.

He follows me out into the hall and his deep voice stops me. "*Malia.*"

"What?" I bite out, spinning to look at him.

Alex looks at me coolly as he pulls his phone from his back pocket.

We stare at each other for a moment, and I can feel my heart beating all the way to my throat.

"I won't be needing that last guess, so I might as well delete your number now." Each tap on his screen hits me like a punch and I'm sure if he'd look up, he'd see my façade cracking. Because for a moment there, I thought we had *something*. Maybe that was just wishful thinking.

"Great, I'll do the same," I say, and leave him behind.

TWO WEEKS *Later*

"I THOUGHT WE HAD AN AGREEMENT," Coach Michael says, running a hand through his light brown hair.

"I did too, but we got to the gym this morning and the *manchildren* were there, taking up our machines, on our assigned time," I say, getting heated and annoyed for having to explain this for the third time.

"Alex, is this true? Did you mess with their schedule?" Michael asks tiredly.

I turn my glare to the man standing next to me with his hands tucked in the pockets of his athletic pants. He shrugs. *Shrugs*.

My eye twitches and I snap, "Seriously, are you that threatened by me and my team that you need to go out of your way to mess with our schedule?"

"Settle down, it wasn't like that," he says lazily, turning just his head toward me.

"Then what is your deal?" I groan. "First you postpone all our meetings to talk about the agreement, then you take forever to agree to the terms, and now this?"

"Look, Thursday mornings are important for us. We have a ritual, okay? We work out, then we go to brunch as a team. We can't do that if you take over the gym in the morning."

"Seriously? The whole team works out and goes to brunch?" I scoff.

Alex sighs and scowls at me. "No, we do it in groups. It's usually just the first line that comes out on Thursdays."

"First line?" I ask, confused.

"See, I knew you didn't know jack shit about hockey," Alex says, turning and taking a step towards me.

I meet him there, poking a finger to his well-built chest. "I don't need to know anything about it. If you're the one playing it, it must be pretty lame."

"You are the most infuriating person I've ever met," he says, chest heaving. I poke it twice more for good measure, before backing up.

I take a deep breath, schooling my features and say, "Fine."

"What?" Alex and Michael speak at the same time.

"Fine, we'll trade Thursday mornings for Fridays," I say, admiring my blunt nails with nothing but a bit of chipped nail polish on them.

Alex squints his eyes at me and says, "What's the catch?"

"No catch," I say and bat my eyes at him. "But you do owe me a favor."

TWO

Two Months Later

THE WORKOUTS that Coach Jackson is putting us through are gruesome to say the least. I've unintentionally lost ten pounds due to all the stress I'm under, topped with his strict practices and workouts. I sway as I get off the elliptical machine and steady myself against the wall, blinking the white spots away from my vision.

"Is that how you practice—dry heaving against the wall?" Alex's deep voice booms around me and I wince at how loud it is in here. I didn't notice the hockey guys entering the gym, probably because I was too busy focusing on not passing out.

Once I'm sure I won't faint, I straighten up and look around the room. The guys are taking up a variety of machines and weights while my teammates wrap up their cardio. As they walk out of the gym, I notice more than one guy checking out a girl's backside. I also catch Jonie and

Andrea's reciprocating glances and scowl. *Those two never listen.*

I roll my eyes and look at my nemesis. His black hair falls in perfect waves and for the first time, he's not wearing his lucky hat. At least, I assume it's lucky, because he wears it all the damn time.

I squint and lean in close, studying his face. His eyebrows hike up his forehead and I say, "Almost didn't recognize you without your emotional support hat." I jump up on the bench near me and assess him from above. My right hand reaches out and combs through his hair.

Fuck, it's soft, just like I thought it would be. Alex freezes to the spot and I do another comb-through, tugging at the roots a little.

"What are you doing?" he asks, a little breathlessly.

I sigh. What am I doing? Feeling his hair because I've secretly wanted to for the past two months. I recover quickly and say, "Checking to see if you were using that hat to cover your premature male pattern baldness."

At my words, Alex seizes my hand in his much bigger one and pulls it away, taking a step closer to me. His eyes are level with my chest and I don't miss the way he glances at the skin that pokes out of my tight sports bra. I may not have much to work with in that area, but I do know how to make it look good.

I don't realize what he's doing until it's too late. He bends down and throws me over his shoulder, walking me out of the gym.

"Alright, your time's up. Please respect the schedule we worked so hard on agreeing to," Alex says as he roughly sets me back on my feet and slams the glass door shut. I glare at him through the windows, but the asshole just smiles and waves at me.

This is what the past two months have been like. Lots of bickering and catfighting, which has only added to my stress. Not only am I responsible for my team and making sure we have an amazing start to our season next month, but I also have a lot riding on my shoulders. I don't want to disappoint my parents, who have given me all their support, and I don't want to disappoint Jackson.

And Alex—well, he's definitely not helping anything. He's the bane of my freaking existence, even if he is infuriatingly hot. Ever since the day we met, he's been taunting and teasing me relentlessly.

I've never had a nemesis or a rival, but I imagine that's what Alex is to me. And if I were to pinpoint the exact moment I started disliking him with a passion, it would be that day two months ago when he deleted my number. I did the same, of course, but I'm not sure why that small action hurt me so much.

AFTER TAKING A LONG SHOWER, I head to Coach Jackson's office. Recently, my anxiety spikes every time I see a message from him. I've started to learn that he's actually kind of narcissistic. And maybe a little sadistic too, because the meal and workout plans he has for us are absolutely insane. I can barely move some days, but he insists we'll be in the best shape of our lives next month when our season starts.

I've always trusted his judgement and it's gotten me this far—to the professional level. And maybe I just want someone, *anyone*, to believe in me. So I'm going to give this first season my absolute best.

I take a deep breath and knock on the door. Jackson's voice is muffled but I can hear the unmistakably annoyed "Yes" he gives me. I hold my head high as I enter but my steps slow and my gaze narrows, because Alex and his coach, Michael, are sitting in chairs facing Jackson. And there's an extra seat for me to Alex's left.

The legs of the chair scrape against the floor and Alex gives me a lazy tilt of his head, his arms crossed against his broad chest. He's wearing a long sleeve workout shirt today and I'm disappointed I can't stare at his tattoos some more. His black hat is back in place on his head, backwards, and I bite my cheek at the memory of running my hands through that luscious dark hair.

"So, should we get this over with?" Michael asks Jackson, who is standing and pacing behind the desk.

"Right, this might be a bad idea," he mumbles, facing us fully and leaning his arms against the desk. "Marketing has been wanting our two teams to collaborate and they're really pushing for it now that we're getting closer to our season opener. So we came up with a plan. It's something that can help with your image and boost up sales."

Alex's jaw ticks, and I can tell he's annoyed. I'm mostly confused.

"My image is fine," he bites out, face going neutral again.

Jackson snorts as Michael says, "Well..."

Alex whips his head around to look at his coach, eyebrows pulled together. "What the hell does that mean?"

"How many suspensions did you get this season alone, Alex? And we're only a couple months in." Michael speaks quietly, but my ears perk up and I straighten in my seat. Alex shoots me a glance from the corner of his eye and his face is stony.

So I do something I think will annoy him—I smirk. "Are you saying there was more than one suspension? Why doesn't that surprise me?"

Alex opens his mouth to no doubt tear me a new one, but Michael stops him. "Look, I'm not saying that taking penalties and a few suspensions is destroying your career. It's just that some people still see you as a—well—"

"Jackass?" I supply.

"Rabble-rouser?" Jackson says with a twitch of his lips.

"Hothead," Michael finishes mildly.

I grin wildly at Alex, expecting him to laugh it off, or tell us to fuck off. But he doesn't meet any of our eyes. Shit, he might actually be affected by our comments. I wipe the smile off my face and offer an olive branch, even though I don't owe him anything.

"All jokes aside, Alex is a grown man and he clearly doesn't need the image boost," Michael says. "And I think the Thunderbirds need to focus on the opening game night, not whatever marketing came up with."

"Wrong," Jackson interjects. "You might be the best fucking team out there, but if no one shows up to see you play, then it's all a waste of time. These games aren't televised, and we need to bring in revenue."

I swallow hard and clasp my hands tightly together. He's right.

"So what is this plan?" Alex asks.

Jackson and Michael share a glance.

"Well," Michael says, "marketing thinks that you two should do an interview together, maybe a photoshoot. Talk about how great things have been sharing the arena, how proud you are of your teams, all that."

Is he serious right now? I'll talk up my team any day, but talking about how welcoming the Manticores have been would be a blatant lie.

I look at Alex and he's just as shocked as I am. His eyes are huge and look like they might bug out of his head and if I wasn't so distressed I would find it cute—I mean, irritating.

"Absolutely not," he says, and now I'm indignant. Does he find me so repulsive that he couldn't even stomach the idea of an interview with me?

"Why not?" I ask.

He looks at me like I've grown another head and throws his hands up in exasperation. "Jesus, now's not the time to fight with me. Please tell me you see what a bad idea that is. We can't stand each other."

I roll my eyes. "Well, I don't see why we can't put things aside for a day and—" I fake-gag and Alex looks me up and down. "Pretend to be friends," I finish.

"And if we say no to this insane agreement?" Alex changes the subject, and I glance up at his face, finding his assessing eyes on me.

"You can't."

"And why not, Jackson?" Alex asks, eyes blazing.

"Because the interview and photoshoot are already scheduled with the local newspaper. You'd make it worse by backing out now," Jackson says with an easy smile, knowing he's got us right in the palm of his hand.

My shoulders drop and I can't help but look at Alex, hoping he might find a way out of this. He meets my gaze again and for a second I'm hopeful. But that hope gets squashed when he gives a definitive nod and says, "Fine."

Well, shit.

THREE

One Week Later

I TRY to focus on my breathing, but something feels off. My steps falter and I catch myself before I can get seriously injured on the treadmill. Of course this is the exact moment Alex decides to taunt me.

"Aw, look at you, training. Is all this cardio helping you hit a ball straight?" he snickers, leaning one arm against my machine and propping his head on his fist.

"Fuck off, Alex."

"Wow, that's no way to talk to a *friend*, now, is it?"

"What. Are. You. Going. On. About?" I wheeze each word, pushing through the last of my cardio sprint.

A quick glance at Alex and I'm faced with his shit-eating grin. And then I remember—today is the day of the interview.

Blood rushes to my face and I feel like I might pass out. *Wait, that's not good.* I think Alex asks me a question, but I don't hear it. I hit the emergency stop button on the treadmill and bend over, trying to catch my breath.

A warm palm lands on my lower back and a bottle of water appears in front of me. I stand straighter and take a sip, making eye contact with my nemesis. There's concern in those green eyes, but what right does he have to be concerned?

"Are you okay?" he asks with a frown.

I contemplate telling him how exhausted I've been recently but when I take a moment to think, he continues on.

"Does the sight of me appall you so much you need to heave?"

I nod, taking another sip of water and notice his hand is still on my back. *Solid. Warm.* And now I'm thinking about his big hands on me, in all the right places.

The flush that overtakes my face is for reasons other than exertion. When was the last time I was touched by a man?

Stop, this is not the time to think horny thoughts.

"I might puke, your face is just that—" I shudder and he groans, dropping his hand.

"Whatever, I know you secretly like my face," he says, winking at me.

I don't know if he's trying to make me feel better, but it's oddly working. I take small sips of water and come back to myself while he keeps teasing me, and eventually I feel better.

"Did you actually need something from me?" I ask, using a microfiber towel to wipe the sweat off my face.

"Just doing my daily duty of annoying you before we have to pretend to be civil with one another," he says, taking his hat off to run a hand through his soft hair, then flipping it backwards.

"Well, mission accomplished," I say, voice laced with forced cheer.

Alex considers me for a moment and his face turns serious. I straighten my spine and look up at him. I've never seen this expression on his face, and I'm worried about what he'll say.

"This might actually be the death of me."

"What?" I ask, incredulous.

"Being nice to you might kill me," he says with a smirk, and I smack him in the chest with the towel. *Asshole.*

AN HOUR LATER, I'm showered, dressed up in my nicest business casual attire—a sage green top that highlights my collarbone and khakis paired with four inch heels—and a minimal amount of makeup on. My long brown hair is in a braided crown that Jonie so graciously helped me with and a few of my naturally highlighted strands fall out and frame my face.

I'm the first one in the conference room and I take a moment to close my eyes and let go of the anxiety that comes with doing an interview. Not just any interview, but my first one with a newspaper. With the one guy I can't stand. I twist my head to try and relieve some of the pressure there, but the creak of the door breaks me out of it.

When I open my eyes, Alex is leaning against the doorframe, hands in his pockets, his tattoos on display as his white button up sleeves are rolled up to his elbows. His tree trunk thighs are accentuated by the navy blue slacks he wears and fuck me, what did I do to deserve having this guy as my workplace rival? Looking at his handsome face is torture enough, but this?

Unlike my open ogling, the look Alex gives me is contemplative. It's a look that says, *I like what I see but I don't know what to do about it.* Some of his earlier concern still shows on his face as he silently takes me in. That is until he decides to speak. "Almost didn't recognize you. I expected to find a red-faced goblin."

The scowl that overtakes my face is going to give me permanent wrinkles. "You are such a gentleman. No wonder you're single," I deadpan.

"Who said I was single?" he taunts as he steps in the room and casually plops into the seat next to mine.

My heart stops beating for a second because—what the hell?

He's not single anymore?

Was he ever single?

When he flirted with me and texted me—was he seeing someone?

I frown and avoid the giant next to me, but his words linger. Alex slowly pushes my rolling chair away with his foot, but I'm too zoned out to care or stop his antics. His hand lands on the arm of my chair and he all but yanks me back next to him.

"I can hear your thoughts," he says, leaning close enough for me to get a whiff of his cologne. It's—nice.

Fuck, no, what am I saying?

I rear back, meeting his eyes, which are gleaming with mischief. Why does he always have to tease me so much?

"I highly doubt you can read my thoughts," I say, and cross my arms over my chest.

Alex smirks and leans back in his own chair. "I am, by the way."

"You're what?" I ask, my eyes landing on one of his tattoos. It's a beautiful bouquet of lilies with a name written in cursive alongside it. *Anna*.

"Single."

My eyes snap back to his and he notices me looking at the tattoo. He runs a thumb over it, almost absentmindedly, and says, "I knew it bothered you. Not knowing."

I blink at him, lips parting on a question, "Then who is Anna?"

My gaze stays glued to his face and I catch the shutter in his eyes. There's a flicker of pain—there and gone in a second. I want to push because I'm curious, but something stops me. I shouldn't be nosey. I shouldn't be cataloguing his tattoos and the way the veins in his forearms pop when he clenches his fist, anyway.

Yet I can't help but feel a little hint of disappointment when he shuts down the subject.

"Ready for the interview?"

"Yeah, sure," I say, right as the interviewer knocks on the already open door.

"Well, happy to see you two looking cozy," she says brightly, closing the door and placing her large purse on the table. Alex and I exchange a glance, and I'm surprised to see we're wearing matching incredulous expressions.

For the first time since we met, I feel like we might be on the same side.

TWO DAYS *Later*

"DID YOU SEE IT?" Andrea shrieks as she all but shoves her phone in my face after our workout.

"See what? Your screen is off," I say, shaking my head.

Out of all my teammates, Andrea and Jonie are my best friends and roommates. The three of us went to college together, living in the same dorm, spending essentially every waking moment together. When we graduated and Coach Jackson brought us on to play for the Thunderbirds, we decided to continue living together, renting an apartment within walking distance of the arena.

"Oh, shit, my phone died," Andrea says, pouting down at her phone. "Well, you can pull it up on yours. The newspaper posted the video from your interview!"

I groan and finish getting dressed. "I don't think I want to watch it," I say, feeling the nerves swirling in the pit of my stomach. While I thought the interview went fine, I'm worried I was too awkward. That I didn't talk my team up enough. And it didn't help that Alex turned his charm to a whole other level for the interviewer, becoming a completely different person right in front of my eyes.

"What don't you want to watch?" Jonie asks, coming out of her shower.

"The interview," we say at the same time.

"Malia doesn't want to watch it because she thinks she was outshined by the hockey captain," Andrea says, rolling her eyes at me.

I need to find some new friends that don't immediately see right through me.

Jonie gasps and quickly puts on her clothes, reaching for

her phone. "Oh, I have to see it! And I'm sure you were not outshined."

She pulls up the video and I cringe at the sound of my voice.

"It's been wonderful getting to work with the lovely staff and crew at the arena. Everyone welcomed us with open arms."

Jonie and Andrea crack up at my outright lie and I bury my face in my hands. "No, you need to watch this," Andrea insists, pausing the video and I relent, mostly so I can get this over with.

The camera captured Alex leaning back, a comfortable air about him as he rested an arm on the back of my chair. Meanwhile, my cheeks were red, my posture ramrod straight.

Jonie hits the play button.

"Even the hockey team?"

"Of course," I said, voice pitched higher, a small grimace bleeding into my smile. I'm such a bad liar.

"What would you say your relationship has been like?"

My forced smile was frozen on my face but in contrast, Alex was wearing a fond look, biting his lip as he looked at me.

"Mal and I are thick as thieves, aren't we, sweetheart?" he said, moving his arm around my shoulder and leaning into me.

I relaxed my shoulders and turned my head towards Alex, admiring his handsome features as he lied through his teeth about our non-existent friendship.

His thumb rubbed soothing circles on my shoulder, and I kept stealing glances at him as we took turns answering questions about the facilities, our respective seasons, and how excited we were about the partnership.

"One last question, will you two be attending the fundraising holiday gala?"

"Wouldn't miss it for the world," Alex said with an easy smile, talking about the upcoming auction and how it will help benefit local hockey foundations.

The video ends and both Andrea and Jonie turn their heads slowly to look at me. I frown at the wide-eyed expression I see mirrored on their faces.

"What?" I ask.

"Girl, what is up with the sexual tension in this video?" Andrea asks.

I laugh. "What are you talking about?"

"You all but melted into him when he put his arm around your shoulder. And that look you gave him—" Jonie says, fanning herself "—Lord, is it hot in here?"

"It wasn't just her," Andrea says, going back to the moment where Alex was looking at me fondly. She zooms in on the video and shows it to us. "Why does he look like he wants to yank you over and place you in his lap?"

"That's not—you don't know what you're talking about," I say, my cheeks on fire. *Is that really how we were looking at one another?*

"Okay, we're not the only ones thinking the same thing. Look at some of these comments!"

I grab the phone from her and swipe through. *Oh no.*

OMG they are for sure dating, just look at their body language - @hockeygirly3

Excited for a pro volleyball team! And they are totally banging. - @johnsticksandpucks

Right? Look at the rubs he gives her, and the way she looks at him. This is totally romance book worthy. - @readbookswithal

We want more #Malex content. - @hockeygirly3

"So, is there anything between you two?" Jonie asks.

I swallow and close my eyes tight. I haven't told them about my first interaction with Alex at the café, and I was hoping to put that out of my mind, but I don't think I'll be able to. So I tell them everything about that first day, how he texted me right away, and what led to our animosity.

"So you do have the hots for each other, but you also drive each other crazy," Andrea says, water still dripping from her blond hair.

I shake my head. "Maybe that was the case in the beginning, but the guy is infuriating and entitled. No matter what those comments say, nothing is going on between us. And nothing will," I say, shutting down the conversation.

My roommates look at me with pity and I wave them off as I leave the locker room. Rounding the corner, I come face to face with Coach Jackson.

"Malia, glad you're here. We've been summoned for a meeting."

"Oh, okay."

Jackson leads me to one of the conference rooms on the administrative side of the arena and we walk in on Alex and Michael having a whispered conversation.

"Either of you know what this is about?" Jackson asks and the two men in Manticores athletic attire turn around to face us.

I narrow my gaze on Alex, certain whatever he was whispering had to do with me, but all he does is assess me with those piercing green eyes.

"No idea," Michael mumbles, taking a seat.

"Oh good, you're all here," Nori, the head of marketing, says as she enters the room. Trailing behind her is a young woman who looks to be around twenty-two—the same age as me—with dark brown hair and wide tortoiseshell glasses.

Her blue eyes land on Michael first and her cheeks turn a blazing shade of red. *Huh, someone has a crush.*

"This is Jen. She's the Manticores' new photographer and she's graciously agreed to help us out with our little side endeavor."

"I'm sorry, but we're not sure we know what's going on," Michael says, briefly glancing at Jen and then back at Nori.

"You didn't get my email?" she asks, and looks around the room at our shaking heads. "Hm, well the interview you two did the other day has gotten a lot of traction. And by that, I mean we've gotten not only an uptick in social media following and analytics, but also an uptick in sales—for both your teams."

"The people love Malex," Jen says, smiling at me. Now it's my turn to blush.

Shit. So they know about the comments. Are we in trouble? Is that what this meeting is?

"What the hell is Malex?" the giant hockey player asks, taking a step closer to me. I wonder if it's on purpose, or if he just gravitates towards me now. I blink and mentally curse my roommates for putting these thoughts in my head.

Sighing, I pull up the screenshot of the interview comments section and pass it to him. Alex looks at me with a cute furrow in his eyebrows as he takes my phone. I see the moment he registers that people are talking about us—not just about our sports, but us as a couple.

He swallows and looks at me with wide eyes before mouthing *What the fuck?* I snort a laugh, and Nori breaks us out of our little moment.

Is that what we were having? A *moment*?

"Shut it, Dionis."

"For what? I didn't even say anything."

"I saw you mouthing the words," she says, eyes

sparkling as she takes us in. Alex's whole body is turned towards me as he hands me back my phone, and I pocket it before putting a few spaces between us.

"Look, this whole 'shipping' situation is not something we expected to come out of the interview, but we see it as a good thing," Nori says, crossing her arms and meeting our gazes head on. "I want you to keep this up, lean into it."

"Into what?" Alex asks and I inwardly groan, realizing what Nori is asking us to do.

"The idea of you two being a couple," she says to him, slowly enunciating each word like he's a kid.

Alex scowls but he's still not comprehending. I save him from the torture and say, "So you want us to fake date?"

He whips his head toward me, gaping and I give him a look that says, *Really, you didn't put two and two together?*

"That's right. Malia, we'll have you go to a few Manticore games, Jen will snap a few pictures of you admiring your 'boyfriend'," she says, adding air quotes around the word *boyfriend*, "then we'll do a photoshoot of the two of you. Maybe you can even join Alex at the Skatefest event—"

"Oh, what about the gala?" Jen pipes up and my stomach flutters. That's a lot of events for us to pretend to be together for.

"Yes!" Nori exclaims, clapping her hands together. "We'll add a few Thunderbirds to the guest list, add a few items on auction. That's a great idea."

"This can't cut into training time or practices," Jackson says.

"Of course not, and to be honest, this would mostly be an undertaking on Malia's side, since she'd have to adjust to Alex's schedule. What do you say, Malia?"

I take a deep breath and look at Coach Jackson. His

expression is hard, but I can see the battle playing in his mind. He wants me to stay focused, but he also wants us to have good attendance. When he meets my eyes, he gives me a subtle nod. Despite his hardass attitude, he wouldn't lead me astray.

Glancing at Alex, I see he's already watching me, lips pursed. Well, if he doesn't like this agreement, then that makes my decision easier.

"All good with me," I say.

"Alex?" Nori asks expectantly.

He holds my gaze for a moment, his thumb rubbing over his wrist. It's a nervous tick I've noticed about him recently and I'm reminded about the tattoo that rests there. I really hope Anna is not his secret girlfriend. And I *really* hope she won't kick my ass.

FOUR

A week later, I walk down the steep steps of the arena with popcorn in one hand, and a very expensive seltzer in the other. No wonder people don't want to come to our games, this is highway robbery.

The seat reserved for me is by the glass, to the right of the home players' bench, where I can easily be photographed ogling my "boyfriend". I got here early since I'm not a big fan of crowded areas. My ticket got me through the season member area, which was much faster and easier to get through security.

I look up at the JumboTron and notice there's a 10-minute countdown, but the arena is mostly empty and no players are in sight, so I have no idea what it's counting down to. Truth is, I know nothing about hockey. I've never been to a game before, and definitely never watched one in its entirety. It always seemed so pointless, just a bunch of grown men on sharp blades, hitting each other and chasing a puck. What's the fun in that?

I eat my popcorn and watch as people are starting to take their seats, some even walking down to the glass. There are young girls with their phones out, ready to take videos I assume, and kids with signs that say *Candy for a puck?* and *My first hockey game.* I smile as I realize that there must be some kind of fan interaction about to happen. I love to see that.

The clock winds down and the announcer lets us know that the Manticores are about to take the ice for their warmups. Huh. I guess that's not too different from what we do in volleyball.

The crowd starts to cheer and turn towards the tunnel to my left, where the crew made a tower of pucks on the shorter wall. The goalie is the first one out on the ice in his massive equipment—*How can he even move in that?*—and he knocks over the tower as the kids around me cheer. I put my seltzer and popcorn under my seat and stand up too, wanting to see what all the fuss is about. As I look slightly down to the tunnel, Alex looks up and our gazes meet right as he's about to hit the ice. It's only for a second, but I can tell something is different about him. He seems to be buzzing with excitement as he skates around and takes a few shots at the net.

I try to look at other players, I really do—but Alex is so magnetic and moves so gracefully on those skates, that I can't tear my gaze away from him. They run some kind of drill, lining up against the wall and passing pucks back and forth, waiting for their turn to take a shot at the goalie.

When I least expect it, Alex skates up to my side of the glass and shoves his body hard into it, startling me and making me jump a mile high. I glare at him, thinking he did it just to scare me, but he's waving at the kid sitting to my right, and—god forbid, is that a smile? I didn't think he was capable of feeling any emotions, and yet his entire face is transformed. He looks...lighter. Happier.

I was so busy looking at Alex that I didn't notice the kid sitting down next to me. He can't be older than 10, and his left leg is in a cast.

The kid waves back enthusiastically and I look back and forth between them. Pointing at Alex, I say, "You like this guy?"

"Are you kidding? The captain's the best!"

"Really?" I ask, sitting back down next to him. "You don't think he's kind of funny looking?"

A sharp rap on the glass makes me look back at Alex who is now glaring at me. Oops, he must have read my lips. I give him my best innocent look and lift a shoulder.

The kid laughs and I turn in my seat, giving him my full attention, and ignoring the 6'5" player who looks even bigger and more massive than usual on his skates.

"Are you here alone?" I ask, looking around for a parent or guardian, but the seats to the right of him are all empty so far.

"My dad's the coach. I always sit here by myself," he says, eyes glued on the ice.

"You're Coach Michael's son?"

"You know my dad?" he asks, looking at me fully. He's cute, with light brown hair and green eyes. I can see the resemblance to Michael in the shape of his nose and curve of his mouth, but his eyes—they're not Michael's, but that color green is one I've seen before.

"Yeah, he's an adjacent work friend. I play volleyball here, so sometimes we run into each other in the arena."

"You're a Thunderbird?" he asks, eyes lighting up.

"Sure am!"

"That's so cool. I can't wait to see you play."

"Yeah? Do you like volleyball?"

"I do. I like all sports, really. I'm Josh, by the way," he

says, sticking out his hand in such a professional way it makes me bite back a smile.

"Nice to meet you, Josh. I'm Malia."

"So, what are you doing at a hockey game?"

"You know, Josh, I'm wondering the same thing," I say, shaking my head and looking back at the ice. "Your friend here, the captain, forced me to come. He's my—" I stop myself, almost saying "nemesis-turned-fake-date", but that's not something a 10-year-old needs to know. Plus, I should probably keep up the ruse anyway. "He's my—boyfriend." The word tastes weird on my tongue and there's a mixture of dread and giddiness battling for control.

Josh looks at me, his eyebrows lost somewhere under his floppy hair. "Really?"

"Yep," I lie, taking a sip of my drink.

Alex chooses that moment to come back to our side of the ice. He drops down on all fours, starting a series of stretches that will be ingrained on my brain for a long, long time. I take a sip of my seltzer to mask my blushing at his hip thrusting. *Seriously, what is he trying to do? Impregnate the ice?*

Josh gives me a rundown of how hockey works after I moronically asked when halftime was going to take place. Apparently, there are three periods and two intermissions in hockey, and with this being an American Hockey League game, the intermissions are filled with fun experiences for fans. Josh is talkative and I'm glad for the company and the lesson, so I share my popcorn with him.

As we wait for the game to start, Coach Michael comes up to the barrier between us and the bench, checking in on Josh.

"Malia, hi," he says, blinking at me like he barely recognizes me. I bet he expected *gym-rat* Malia, not the *girly*

Malia—the one that puts on tight jeans, a nice green top, a leather jacket, and makeup.

I give him my best smile, despite the fact that he's nemesis-adjacent, thanks to Alex. "Hi, Coach Michael. Hope you don't mind that Josh is keeping me company here. I need someone to teach me about hockey."

Josh hobbles over closer to his dad and groans, pointing wildly at me. "Dad, she thought there was a halftime. In hockey. How is she Cap's girlfriend if she knows nothing about the game?"

Michael snorts and smooths his expression before looking at his kid again. "Sometimes, opposites attract, I guess. How is your leg? You should have just stayed home."

Josh crosses his arms and straightens up. "Leg's fine. Barely even hurts anymore." The two of them are locked in a stare-off and I smile as I watch their dynamic. The kid seems to be tough as nails, and funny too. I wonder if he takes more after his mom.

"Alright, go sit back down. I'll see you at the end. Bring Malia down for some food too, okay?"

Josh nods and sits back next to me.

"What was he talking about?"

"There's a dinner after the game where all the staff and players go. It's in one of the big conference rooms. I always go after a game."

"By yourself?"

"Um, yeah," he says, and I can pick up on the shift in his voice. He sounds a little sad.

"What about your mom?"

Josh is quiet for a minute, looking at the JumboTron that shows people around the arena; a couple kissing, kids cheering, and grown men chugging beer.

"She died. Two years ago," he says softly, and my heart breaks for this adorable kid.

"Aw, bud, I'm so sorry."

He gives me a half shrug that seems to say, *What can you do?*, and he brushes it off just as quickly. "It's okay, I don't really remember her that much, which is kind of sad. But my dad is great. And Uncle Alex is always around."

I nod in agreement until I realize he means *my* Alex. Before I can deal with the fact that I referred to my nemesis as *mine*, I say, "Wait, Alex is your actual uncle?"

"Yeah," he nods. "My mom—Anna—was his sister."

"Oh," I say, feeling a pang of sorrow for the three of them. I hadn't realized Alex had a sister, let alone one that passed away. I wonder what the meaning of his tattoo is, if it's some sort of way to honor her with a bouquet of lilies. I frown and think about my little brother. I can't imagine how much that kind of loss would hurt.

We sit in silence for a bit until the team gets properly introduced on the ice and the starting players take their places, Alex being one of them. We all rise for the national anthem and watch something called the "ceremonial" puck drop, where a special guest drops the puck on the ice and the captains of the two teams shake hands.

Except the special guest is not a person, but a rescue dog. Barney, as the JumboTron tells me, is currently chewing on the puck and refuses to let it drop, an action that makes the whole arena chuckle in a collective "Aww."

Alex ends up prying it out of the dog's mouth and ruffling his fur, and Barney retaliates by jumping up on Alex's leg. The whole scene is so wholesome that I can't justify this man and the man I bicker with every day being the same person. Though lately, I've been seeing some glimpses into his softer side.

"Okay, so once the puck drops, they'll play until the whistle goes off or until someone scores. It's very fast paced, but just try to keep your eyes on the puck," Josh says.

I nod along and follow the puck as best as I can, as fans cheer all around me, chanting "Let's go Manticores!" My eyes stay glued to Alex every time he has a shift and I don't know what I expected—probably that he'd start a fight with someone right away, since that's what he's known for, but he is truly incredible out there. He skates with such grace and confidence, and he handles the puck so easily, passing it to his teammates and catching it back.

I'm so mesmerized by it all—the gameplay, the intensity, the love these fans have for the game—that when the refs send Alex to the penalty box for what Josh tells me is a bogus high stick, I'm out of my seat and booing with the rest of the fans. Josh bangs on the glass and I do the same, yelling out, "Ref, you suck!"

The play is stopped and Alex is arguing with one of the refs, but eventually he relents and sits down, shaking his head. He takes off his helmet and shakes his sweaty hair and I swear, for a moment, as I'm banging on the glass, he locks eyes with me.

I quickly sit back down and cross one leg over the other, the picture of indifference, but it's too late. The grin that overtakes his face says that he noticed me. *Damn it.*

THE MANTICORES WIN 4-2 and the excitement in the arena is palpable as we make our way down the escalator and to one of the conference rooms. The rest of the game got more and more exciting, and I even got to see a fight right in front of my seat. Alex wasn't involved, and I don't know if that made me more or less excited about it.

I've never cared for the violence, but the truth is, after how frustrating some of the plays were, I can see how a fistfight helped not only the players blow off steam, but also helped relieve some of the tension in the arena. The intermissions were really fun too. Between having Cory, the Manticores mascot, paying our seats a visit, and the ice crew throwing T-shirts into the stands, I was genuinely pleased with the whole experience.

"I'm starving," my new friend says, hobbling around on his crutch.

"Hey, what happened to your leg? How did you break it?" I ask, curiosity getting the best of me.

"Skateboarding accident a couple of weeks ago. The cast should be coming off soon," Josh says, nodding to the security guy in front of the large door in front of us. The guy checks my badge, clearly knowing the little kid I'm with since he's here every game. I push open the door and once I do, Josh swiftly moves past me towards the giant table of food.

"Can you hold this?" he says, handing me his crutch and loading up a plate of food for himself, hopping around.

"Want some help?" I chuckle.

He hesitates for a second, looking at me over his shoulder. "Yes. Can you grab me some juice and garlic bread?"

I hand him back his crutch and do as he says, shaking my head at him when I find him sitting at a table a moment later, face deep in a plate of pasta. "Are you in a rush or something?"

He groans and rolls his eyes and the gesture reminds me so much of my little brother that I smile and laugh.

"I just love food. Are you gonna have some?"

I glance over at the table of food. It all smells amazing and I'm hungry, but if I eat any of those carbs, I'm going to have to work out twice as hard tomorrow. I grimace and give a head shake. "I'm not that hungry."

"You'll regret that later. Once the players come out here, there won't be anything left."

"Ha! You may be right," I say, and fix myself up a small plate of food, letting myself indulge a little. I take my seat next to my new little friend as we eat in companionable silence.

"You're not what I would've expected," he says a few minutes later, pushing his empty plate away.

"What do you mean?"

"Well, Uncle Alex never brings anyone to games, or any other team events," he says, brow furrowing and mouth turning down. "The one time he did, his date made him leave early and she didn't want to hang out with me."

"How rude!" I exclaim dramatically. Josh gives me a small smile and it lights me up. "Well, Cap isn't the smartest fella out there, so I'm not surprised by his choice of women," I say, and I realize that's also a dig at myself, since I'm supposedly dating him. I quickly add, "That is, until he met me, of course."

Josh's smile turns more into a grin as he looks over my shoulder. *Oh boy.*

I slowly turn around and look up, up, up, at the team captain, towering over me. His arms are crossed and his hair is damp, but he's looking like a million bucks in a cream colored button-up, with a black sports jacket on his arm and dark khakis that hug his muscular thighs just right.

He looks positively delicious.

That is until he opens his mouth.

"I can't even imagine what you've poisoned his mind with," he says, green eyes bright and focused wholly on me.

"You're one to talk. I'm sure every bad word he knows he learned from you, *Uncle Alex*."

His lips twitch and Josh pipes up to say, "Actually, I learned it all from my dad. He's pretty unfiltered."

I laugh and turn back to him at the table. "Do you want some more food? I can grab it for you."

Eyes lighting up, he says, "Yes, please. Extra bread."

"How can kids eat so much? It's like his stomach is a bottomless pit," I say under my breath as I walk by Alex.

He shrugs and follows me to the food table where players are already lined up and pilling pasta on their plates. I take a moment to take in my enemy. Not only does he look good, but there's something about his demeanor that I don't usually get to see. Maybe it's because he's not scowling or teasing me for once.

Alex looks over at the kid and smiles softly and I almost trip on my feet when I see that gorgeous pull of his lips. "He's pretty active when he doesn't break any limbs."

"I'm sure he is. He seems to be into every sport imaginable."

"Yeah, hopefully he chooses to go into hockey, otherwise his dad might lose his will to live."

"Oh, whatever, maybe he'll go to play professional volleyball," I quip, smiling broadly.

Alex snorts and I whip my head around to glare at him, except I'm met with the column of his throat instead. He leans in and whispers, "Trust me, hockey is in that kid's blood."

I roll my eyes and take a step back, trying to put some distance between us. Because the smell of him is starting to clog my senses and I'm thinking about that day at the gym when he put his palm on the small of my back and—

"What, no comeback?" Alex boops—*fucking boops* my nose—and bumps me out of the way so he can make himself a plate.

I stew in silence for a few moments, thrown off by our new dynamic, and contemplating why it's changing. And then I remember that I'm supposed to be his fake girlfriend tonight. I plaster on a huge smile and grab his forearm, holding on so tight that my blunt nails are digging in.

Alex looks down, eyebrows lifting higher and higher on his forehead. "What are you doing?"

"Spending time with my loving *boyfriend*, clearly."

He snorts, but doesn't push me away. "How come you're still here, by the way? Don't you have someone else to torture with your presence?" he asks as we walk back to the table arm in arm. He doesn't say it with malice, but my stomach still drops all the same at the feeling of being unwanted. This isn't my team or my family. So what am I doing here?

I try to slide my arm out of his as we place the plates down on the table, but he doesn't let me. Turning to me, he notices the tears I'm trying to blink back and for a moment, he's quiet.

I look around the table just so I don't have to meet his gaze. All the seats are taken by players and Coach Michael, who is now sitting next to his son. "Look at that," I say, trying to muster up a smile, "no seats left. Guess that's my cue to *torture* someone else."

Alex frowns down at me. "I didn't mean—"

I don't give him a chance to finish his sentence. Clearing my throat, I say, "Nice to see you again, Coach Michael.

And lovely to meet you, Josh. I appreciate the lesson in hockey terminology."

Josh laughs and mutters, "As long as you never utter the words halftime and hockey together in the same sentence, my job here is done."

I smile, but it quickly dims as the entire table of players starts hooting and hollering, making fun of my lack of knowledge.

"Hey! No one can make fun of my *girlfriend* except for me, got it?" Alex scolds his teammates and the whole table goes silent. "That includes you, Josh."

"Sorry, Uncle Alex," the kid says, twirling his fork through the second serving of pasta I brought him.

"It's not me you have to apologize to."

"Sorry, Malia." Josh shoots me an apologetic smile and I give him a reassuring one back.

"It's okay," I say, feeling bad that the poor kid is getting disciplined because of me. "I appreciate you teaching me the proper terms."

Alex lets go of my arm and walks to the corner of the room, grabbing two more chairs.

"Sit," he says, green eyes pinning me to the spot.

After that display of solidarity, I have no choice but to obey as he makes room for me at the table.

FIVE

I make the mistake of looking straight at the light for the billionth time and I rapidly blink the white spots forming in my vision.

I'm wearing my signature leather jacket again today, this time paired with an olive turtleneck underneath that brings out the green flecks in my hazel eyes. My high waisted jeans are ripped at the knee but flare wide at the bottom, my chunky boots making me seem taller than my usual 5'5" frame.

Alex bounces his knee in the seat next to me and it makes the whole aisle shake. I scowl, taking him in for the first time since we arrived at the arena for our photoshoot. He looks like he shaved this morning, and I mentally chide myself for even noticing. *What is it about him that makes me so drawn to him?*

His normally green eyes have a hint of blue in them today, courtesy of the navy button-up shirt he's wearing. His tattoos are peeking out of his sleeves a little each time he moves, and I sit up a little straighter, crossing my legs. His attractiveness is starting to bother me, but more than that, it's my reaction to him that annoys me.

"Almost thought you wouldn't show up today," he says, leaning into my seat so others around can't hear the conversation.

Twisting around to meet him, I say, "Why?"

Alex watches my face intently, his eyes meeting mine in a challenge. "You were quiet at dinner and then you skipped the other two home games. I figured you were bothered by something and that you'd changed your mind about the whole arrangement."

I hear the camera click again and turn my head towards the photographer. Didn't she have to adjust something? We haven't posed yet. She hesitates on the next picture and says, "I want to try taking some candid pictures of you two, so just act like you normally would when you're together."

We're supposed to be acting like a couple. Wrapping my hands around his throat and squeezing is probably not what Jen is looking for here.

Alex softly snorts, saying, "I don't think she wants pictures of you strangling me."

I bite my cheek, trying hard not to laugh. How did he know what I was thinking?

Taking a deep breath, I turn my head back towards Alex. From everyone's point of view, it probably looks like we're whispering secrets to one another, heads bent together, my body constantly in tune with his.

"I didn't change my mind, by the way," I say, meeting his gaze head on.

Alex raises one eyebrow at me and the corners of his lips twitch. "You sure?"

"I want people to come see the Thunderbirds play. If

the price I need to pay is fake dating you for a bit, then so be it."

His smile fades at my words, and I want to know what he's thinking. But then we're interrupted by Jen.

"Okay, can you guys do something that looks at least a little bit couple-y?" she asks, pointing at us frustratingly. "These pictures look lifeless, to be frank. I'm not here to take your headshots."

I blush and stand up, adjusting my ponytail and the few strands of hair that are loose around my face. Without preamble, I take a step towards Alex and drape myself over his lap, trying not to notice the hard muscles flexing as he adjusts to my weight. He lets out a grunt of surprise behind me as his hands come to grip my waist, moving me in a position that is more comfortable for the both of us.

I smile at the photographer and she snaps a few pictures of us like that. I can tell she wants more, so I lean into Alex, turning more in his lap and putting my arm around his shoulder. His soft exhale hits the skin of my neck, and I shiver. I swing my legs up over the seat I was in a moment ago and loop both my arms around his neck. Alex's left hand stays rooted to my hip, but his other lands on my exposed knee.

I try my best to look like I'm happy, but the truth is, I'm miserable on the inside. Because I had finally accepted the fact that Alex was nothing more to me than a nemesis, a workplace rival, and now—I have to pretend he's so much more.

Jen tells us to keep the pose as she tries a few different angles, so I stay in his lap, doing my best not to fidget. He's solid and warm under me, oddly relaxed. If this was a completely different circumstance, I would want his body to wrap around mine and just—*do something*—anything, really. I'd probably be happy with just a hug.

Am I that starved for attention?

I let my eyes roam all over his face, noticing a couple of beauty marks and a scar above his right eyebrow. His nose looks just a little bit crooked, like maybe it was broken one too many times. And his eyes—god, I could lose myself in them. Alex meets my gaze head-on and gives me the same kind of intense perusal I gave him, and I can't help but wonder if he likes what he sees. He did once, enough to text me within an hour of getting my number.

Someone asks a question, but I'm so enthralled by studying Alex that I miss it. The soft squeeze of his hand on my knee brings me out of the reverie and I look around, startled.

"We can move on to the next spot," Jen says, heading down the stairs and onto the main floor of the arena. I stand up and almost trip on my feet, but Alex steadies me with a hand around my middle. We look at one another in silence before he lets me go and follows the photographer and I have no choice but to do the same.

The ice has been covered for volleyball practice today, and there's a backdrop set up for us with both our team logos on it. I let Jen handle me as she figures out what pose will work best, and I try to avoid Alex as much as I can when the camera is not pointed at us. I feel unsettled around him.

Jen offers me a volleyball and I spin it around in my hands just to have something to do. She holds out a pair of skates for Alex to take. They look way too small for him, and he stares at them with such disgust that I burst out laughing.

"What the hell is this?" he asks.

"Props. You're gonna put them on your shoulder, let them hang from their laces. Or hold them up."

"That's the stupidest thing I've ever heard," he grumbles, and scowls at me as I'm doubled over in laughter.

"Well, this is the only prop we have for you, so..." Jen trails off, shrugging.

I wipe a tear from my eye and say, "Bet you wished you played a regular game with a ball right about now, huh?"

Alex narrows his eyes at me before giving me a slow, Cheshire Cat smile. I don't see it coming, but the next moment, he grabs the ball from my hand and holds it up over his head. "What, like this ball?"

My mouth drops open as I do the one thing I shouldn't —reach on my tiptoes for it—only to immediately land back on my feet. "What are you, five? You're just gonna steal my toy?"

Alex smirks down at me and my nostrils flare with irritation. "If it makes you angry, then yes."

"You're such a child sometimes," I grumble, and pretend to give up, only to jump back up, smacking his bicep when I can't reach again. *Why is it rock-hard?*

"Aw, is this too high for you? What are you gonna do about it, *sweetheart*?" he taunts. *God, does he ever shut that pretty mouth of his?*

Instead of jumping up and down and looking like a fool in the pictures Jen is taking of us, I come up with another tactic. I take a step closer to Alex and he twists his body so that one side is closer to me, while the other is stretched away, holding the ball high. I smirk, meeting his eyes. I got him right where I want him.

He started this game with the wrong person. Because I play dirty when I want to win. With how close he is to me, I easily wrap both my arms around his neck and jump into his arms. My legs hook around the small of his back and I take in his surprised face. On reflex, he wraps his free hand around me, holding me close.

We stand there, frozen, until I hear the click of the camera once again. *I should probably move.*

Leaning in, I whisper, "If you're gonna play dirty, then so am I."

Alex's pupils are blacker than I've ever seen them, but I don't stop to analyze it. I climb him like a tree, pushing myself up higher in his arms until I reach the ball in his hand and snatch it away. With a look over my shoulder at Jen, I smile triumphantly, then toss the ball aside.

Alex's hands grip me tight as he repositions me in his arms so I'm once again level with his face.

"Well played. Don't worry though, I'll get you next time," he says in a low voice. *Like a promise.*

I swallow hard and disentangle myself from his arms, straightening out my jacket and running a shaking hand over my shirt. Alex remains stoic and I'm a little annoyed that he's not affected by me the same way I am by him.

Was his skin not on fire where my fingers touched the back of his neck?

Did his breath not catch when I jumped into his arms?

Just when I think I might lose my mind about him, I notice his fists clenching and unclenching, like he might want to reach out again and hold me longer. And I don't know if the thought of being in his arms again excites me or terrifies me further.

How am I supposed to fake feelings for him, when my all-too-real attraction is simmering below the surface?

SIX

I stare at my phone, swiping through the photoshoot results. Somehow, Jen managed to make us look like we more than tolerate one another. The pictures look sexy, with me sitting in Alex's lap in one shot and wrapped around him like a koala in another. I bite my lip and stupidly think that we might have made a really good couple if we didn't despise one another.

There's something about the way he's looking at me, so intently, that makes me think he wants to devour me whole. Or maybe he just wants to murder me. Could go either way.

A text reminder from Jackson tells me that I need to be on time at the outdoor ice rink. The Manticores have this tradition called Skatefest where the players come out and skate with fans, alternating who is out on the ice. Alex is slotted for 4 p.m. and I've been instructed to show up and act the part of doting girlfriend, because local news stations will be around, covering the event. I silence my phone and put it back in my pocket, taking in the sights around me.

The park in the center of town is decked out in a myriad of Christmas lights and decorations, from inflatable elves and snowmen to a large sleigh next to the skating rink that kids are climbing on. And beyond the park, a 15-foot tree is lit up and surrounded by people of all ages, taking pictures. I stand there for a moment, taking in the sight and smiling like a fool.

I didn't grow up with any of this in Hawaii—not the snow, not the cold weather, and definitely not the pines and spruces. All of a sudden, I'm hit with a pang of homesickness as I remember the traditional luau with my parents, and how my brother would play carols on the ukulele. I make a mental note to call them later when I return to my apartment.

"You're late." A familiar deep voice snaps me out of my daze and I plaster a smile on as I turn around and face Alex. He's frowning at me, and it's infuriatingly cute and intimidating at the same time. Sometimes I don't know if I'm actually attracted to this neanderthal or if I'm just horny.

"Sorry," I say, lifting my chin and widening my eyes in an innocent look. He rolls his eyes at my bullshit apology and thrusts out his hand. There's a cup of something hot and I wearily take it from him, pulling the lid off and giving it a sniff. It smells like peanut butter and chocolate and my mouth instantly waters. I love peanut butter. How did he know?

"Let's get this over with," he mumbles and turns towards the tent that's set up by the skate rental box.

I stick my tongue out at his back, but follow him anyway. "What's with you today?"

"Nothing," he snaps as he pulls up a flap of the tent. I stop in my tracks, a little shocked at his attitude. I don't think I've ever seen him downright mad.

Alex turns back, running a hand down his ragged face, and I notice the circles under his eyes. "I'm sorry, I'm just not looking forward to this. My—" He stops, looking at me, debating if he should tell me.

I keep my expression open, wondering if he will.

"My sister died two years ago around this time, and she worked for our organization, doing local outreach. This event was her baby, and I'm kind of dreading doing it again without her," he says, shoulders caving in.

"Alex, I'm so sorry," I mumble, not knowing what else to say.

"Don't take my attitude personally, it's just—a lot to deal with right now."

"I'm sure. Do you want to cancel our appearance on the ice? I can fake sickness," I say, forcing a cough.

Alex gives me the briefest smile but shakes his head. "No, I can't let people down."

I nod along, understanding the feeling well. He pulls the flap higher and we head inside. The tent is cozy, a group of people hanging out behind a plastic table, selling Manticores merch and handing out hot cocoa.

I look down at my fancy cup that looks nothing like the Styrofoam one on the table. Alex clocks the movement and slightly purses his lips. "Yours came from the food truck across the street."

Oh. Well, that's thoughtful of him.

"Thanks," I say, taking a sip of the delicious cocoa.

He grabs us both skates from a box under the table and we take a seat on the plastic chairs in the corner of the tent. I struggle with the laces of the hockey skates, having only ever used rental ones that were much easier to put on.

Alex, on the other hand, finishes putting his on in record time. When he sees me struggling, he kneels down in front of me. I'm so stunned that all I do is stare at him, skates forgotten.

His black hair peeks out of his red Manticores hat, and it looks *thick*. There's an impulse to take off his hat and run my fingers through it to check if it's just as soft as the last time, but I fist my hands at my side and pray I won't do something as stupid as that.

"Tap the heel of the skate against the ground a couple times."

"Why?"

"Because you want your heel to be firmly in place," he says, matter-of-fact. "How about you trust the pro hockey player on this one, yeah?" He smiles and I bite my lip, whacking the blade against the black carpet. As soon as I do, Alex reaches out and takes my foot in his hands, securing it between his meaty thighs. My eyes are fixed on the image in front of me, slowly following his hands as he tightens the laces with so much precision, moving from one skate to the other.

"Is this a bad time to tell you that I'm a terrible skater?" I say, intently watching the way his long fingers hook and pull from bottom to top.

Alex stops midway to forming a loop and looks up at me with his gorgeous green eyes. I mean, *how* are they such a lovely shade of green?

"Haven't you lived here for years now?" he asks, eyes narrowing.

I chew the inside of my cheek and admit, "Yeah but I rarely went out. I've only skated a couple of times."

"Why didn't you go out more?" Alex asks with genuine curiosity.

I shrug lamely, finishing off my hot cocoa. "I was too focused on volleyball, on school. I didn't want to fail." I laugh and shake the gloomy regrets out of my head. "So yeah, I never learned to properly skate."

"Well, I skate for a living, so you can trust me not to let you fall," Alex says, standing up and offering me a hand. I take it and let him lead me down the mat to the rink.

As we're leaving the tent, Jackson steps in front of us. I'm confused as to why he's here. This is a Manticores event, and besides me, no one else from the volleyball team is in attendance.

"You two better sell it out there," Coach says. "The whole point of this fake dating arrangement was to boost both your images and capitalize on it. Get more ticket sales."

So that's why he came. He doesn't think I'm doing enough in this agreement and wants to push me to do more.

"Every time I see you, you just scowl at one another." Jackson says, looking down at me with disapproval. "You need to—"

"How about you let us decide what we do or don't do about our supposed relationship?" Alex's hand squeezes mine and I take that as a small sign of solidarity. He doesn't like this situation any more than I do. As he takes a step forward, Jackson has no choice but to move aside and let us pass.

"Is the fact that we're here together not enough?" I quietly ask.

Alex looks back at me but shakes his head. "There's no point in talking about that here. We'll figure it out."

I nod and follow his lead, fingers flexing in his. Looking around the rink, there are people out there already, skating around and waving at Alex. A few people are taking out their phones and snapping pictures, floppy-haired teenagers backslapping one another once they realize who Alex really is.

I take my first step on the ice and my feet immediately

slide from under me. Even as I flail, Alex's hand is steady in mine, and he easily pulls me closer to him.

"Just take it one foot at a time," he says softly. I'm shocked speechless, but I listen to Alex the whole time. Especially as he leads me around the rink and teaches me how to skate properly, all the while showing off, skating backwards, doing crossovers, and taking some fast laps with teenagers when I ask for a break.

For some reason I didn't expect him to be this *nice*.

To other people, of course.

He's still a menace to me, his hockey adversaries, and probably most of society. But as he's signing jerseys and hats, a small smile on his lips, and his hand holding mine while we skate, I don't think he's as bad as he paints himself to be. And I think even though he dreaded this event, he's still finding some joy in it.

As more Manticores players take the ice, we realize an entire hour has passed. Alex pulls me to the side and stops us both in place with a hand on my waist.

"Do you see those photographers over there?" he asks in a low voice.

I look over my shoulder and notice a group of people with cameras around their necks, Jen being one of them.

"We never discussed the details of our fake dating arrangement. Is kissing allowed?" he asks, and I whip my head back around. His eyes are glued to my lips like he can already taste me. "If so, those photographers are going to get a real kick out of it," he says, one corner of his mouth pulling up.

My heart drops somewhere in the vicinity of my stomach. *Of course, this is all for show.*

He's giving Jackson what he wants, those photographers

were probably sent over by him. I look around the small rink before resting my gaze somewhere south of his eyes.

"So, do I have permission to kiss you?" he asks, squeezing my waist.

I nod meekly, with much less enthusiasm than either of us probably expected. Alex places his cold fingers on my face, tilting my chin up to meet his eyes. "I need your words, please."

This might be the first time in his life he's uttered the word *please*, so I give in and say, "Yes, kiss me."

His mossy green eyes pierce me to the spot as he slowly leans in, and I meet him halfway. His mouth is so soft against mine, tentative and searching. It's definitely not what I expected from this man. I expected him to shove his tongue down my throat and grab my ass, showing those photographers that I belong to him. And while that is one hundred percent caveman behavior and I would never stand for it, why am I the slightest bit disappointed?

While I'm in my own thoughts about this kiss, Alex pulls back suddenly and frowns down at me. "I thought you said you were fine with the kiss," he says.

"I am," I squeak out, scrunching my eyebrows right back at him.

"Then why are you not kissing me back?" he says, scowling at me some more.

Oh. I guess I was so caught up on how he wasn't kissing me the way I expected him to that I didn't reciprocate. "Sorry, I was just—overthinking," I say, opting for some honesty.

Alex scrutinizes me for another moment, flakes of snow settling on the black hair that's poking out of the Manticores winter hat. His words take me by surprise as he all but growls, "If you're thinking at all while I'm kissing you, then I'm not doing it right."

I can't do anything but stare at him with wide eyes, because what the hell do I say? *The kissing was fine, but I want it rougher?* I try to keep my face blank, but I get the sense that he can read me anyway. Somehow, he always does.

Alex gives a small nod, almost like he's convincing himself of something. "Permission to do it again?" he asks, already leaning in.

"Granted," I say, and lean into him more, waiting for that tender press of his lips to mine again. Except—it doesn't come. Alex bends down and his hands go around my thighs as he lifts me clean off the ice and sits me down on the edge of the sideboard. My arms immediately go around his neck in fear of falling backwards as he steps closer between my legs.

"Don't worry, sweetheart, I got you," he assures me, with a tight grip on my waist, right before he crushes his lips to mine.

This kiss is nothing like the one before. All traces of tenderness are gone as Alex kisses every inch of my mouth, tugging at my lower lip with his teeth. And when he licks the seam, I forget my own name and open up to him. His tongue is eager and exploring as I move my fingers to the back of his head and thread them through the soft black hair, tugging at the roots. The man is hungry and the only thing that can satiate him is the taste of me.

For a moment, we forget that we're in public.

At an outdoor skating rink.

At a family friendly event.

We break apart when a group of teenagers start

hollering and hooting at us. We're both panting and our lips are red and swollen. But I can't bring myself to look at him, so I settle my gaze on the lit-up Christmas tree behind him.

Fuck. That may have been the hottest kiss of my life.

SEVEN

Day and night, the image of Alex with cheeks rosy from the cold and lips swollen from kissing me plagues my thoughts, my dreams, my every waking moment. It's frankly annoying. And it needs to stop.

I've avoided him the past two days, not knowing what I would do or say the next time I see him. Is he gonna see it in my expression? How much I want him?

I'm not listening to what Jackson is telling me right now, which is next-level bad. There's nothing worse than being distracted around my coach. He slams his hand down on the desk to get my attention and I flinch a little.

"Hey! What's going on?" Alex says gravely from behind me. My reaction is immediate, toes curling in my running shoes and spine straightening. I do my best not to glance at him, knowing that he's probably looking delicious in his athletic shorts and T-shirt, the black ink on his arms on full display.

"Dionis, thanks for coming. I've got some updates. And you—" he says, pointing at me "—pay attention. It's like your head is in the fucking clouds lately."

My cheeks redden and I stare at the floor as Alex steps up closer to me. It feels like a shield and for once, all I want is to let the anxiety and stress coiling inside me go and lean into him. But that's ridiculous.

I can feel his eyes roaming over me, but I don't dare to meet them. When he turns his attention back to Jackson, he says in a hard tone, "I don't have long, what's this about?"

"I need you two on your best behavior on December twenty-sixth for the fundraising gala. And also, Malia, you need to be at the Manticores game on New Year's Eve," Jackson says.

For a second, I think I've misheard him. Jackson has access to my calendar, he knows I'm planning to go back to Hawaii right after the gala and return before the season starts.

I'm shocked for a second, until I realize he's doing this on purpose. Like every other time he's influenced my decisions and guilted me into staying when all I wanted was to see my family.

And now I'm just angry. Because what the hell? I'm supposed to drop everything and follow Alex's schedule, being in attendance at all his games? It doesn't matter how well he kisses me, or how nice his green eyes are. Why should I just drop all my plans for this?

"I have tickets to go home for a couple weeks," I say stiffly. Out of the corner of my eye, I can see Alex glancing at me, arms folded across his chest.

Don't.

Don't think about that scorching kiss.

How can I not when I can still feel it tingling on my lips?

That night ended abruptly after our kiss and I practically bolted off the ice. It wasn't my finest moment, but even if I wanted to open the can of worms and talk to him about it, I don't know how. What would I even say?

We're fake dating and you kissed me because the photographers were there, but that kiss felt anything but fake. I think I want you in a way that I've never wanted anyone, but I also kind of hate your guts because you're always messing with me and it's fucking with my head.

"So change them. Whatever you gotta do," Jackson says in a harsh tone, breaking me out of my spiraling thoughts.

"I can't change them. I haven't seen my family in over a year," I say, panic spiking. *Oh god, my family will be crushed.*

"Maybe you should have thought things through, then. You can't be going on vacation right before your season starts. That's just unprofessional, Malia." I breathe hard through my nose and try to calm down so I don't snap at him, or worse, cry. Because there's nothing I can do. There is too much riding on this, on me, to start off the season with a bang, and I'll have to cancel my plans. I was worried the distance would be too much when I moved here, and it turns out I was right. My parents are going to be crushed.

I want to tell Jackson he's being unreasonable, but there's no compromising with him. All he cares about is the money we bring in, and how, as the face of the Thunderbirds, I need to do everything he says.

I hold back the tears that threaten to spill, mumble some kind of acknowledgment in return, and bolt out of the office, leaving both Jackson and Alex behind.

I'm hoping I can run straight for the doors before anyone can see me cry, but no such luck. The tears spill down my face, my body starts shaking, and I need to duck into a supply closet so I can panic in peace.

I close the door with shaky hands and move to the

nearest shelf, gripping it hard with one hand and muffling my sobs with the other. It doesn't take long for my legs to give out and for me to slide down and sit on the floor. I pull my legs in and bury my head between my knees, trying to catch my breath and stop crying.

Why have I let Jackson dictate my schedule for so long? Do I have to give up everything—my family included—to have my dream of playing professional volleyball?

I don't realize the door has opened until I hear shifting and look over, seeing Alex sitting on the floor next to me, his back to the wall. I am mortified beyond measure, and fucking *angry*.

Angry at him, angry at Jackson, angry at myself.

"Leave, Alex," I say, with less snip than I would like.

"What happened back there?" he asks.

I shake my head and look up at the ceiling, trying to control all these feelings inside. "Nothing happened, I just want to be alone."

"If nothing happened, then why are you crying?" he asks, gentler than I've ever heard him. It makes me want to lash out at him.

"Why the hell do you care?" I bite out. "All you've done the last few months is make my life miserable." I roughly wipe the tears off my face, but my chin quivers again and more tears spill out. I'm being a bitch, and I know it.

Alex doesn't say anything, just sits there next to me, legs spread and feet planted on the dirty floor. He clasps his hands between his knees and just waits for me to speak.

To tell him why I'm crying, I realize. He doesn't touch me, doesn't offer any comfort. Not that I expect him to.

And I don't know if it's his presence that makes me calmer somehow, or the fact that he's asking without pushing me to answer, but surprisingly I give in. "Jackson always does this. I think he means well, he wants us—me—to succeed, but sometimes it's just too much," I say, sniffling.

I look over and Alex is wholly focused on me, his mossy green eyes looking darker in this shabby closet. He nods for me to continue, and once I wipe the rest of my tears off, I say, "He thinks the sport should be my sole focus. The personal training he's put me through the last six months has been absolutely insane.

"I wanted to invite my parents over the summer when my mom wasn't teaching and she could travel, but he said it wasn't wise, that I wouldn't be able to focus on training. That I needed to get my head in the game. When I insisted they should visit, he personally called them and told them I didn't need this kind of distraction. So they felt bad and ended up staying home."

Alex's fists are clenching so hard I think he might be losing circulation in his fingers. Is he angry at me or for me? I don't say anything else for a moment, I just stare in his direction and eventually he says, "Why did you just *take* it back there? Why not tell him to fuck off and that there would be other opportunities for us to promote our teams?"

I sigh tiredly. "Because it wouldn't have made a difference. He has access to my calendar, so he *knew* I had a trip planned and didn't care. I'm sure he did it on purpose."

More tears spill down my face. Why can't I fucking stop crying? This is so humiliating. And yet, Alex is still here and he doesn't seem to be laughing at me.

"Is there maybe more to it than just Jackson being an ass?" he asks quietly.

I relent and nod at him, watching the tattoos peeking out of his sleeves. "I really miss my family. I haven't seen them in over a year and between my schedule and the time difference, I barely get to talk to them or video call as it is."

The guilt of talking to my parents less and less keeps eating away at me. I curl back into myself and quietly let more tears fall. I whisper, "I'm just so *homesick*."

I do my best to control my breathing, but I just end up making it worse to the point I'm sobbing again and shaking. I hear Alex move and I think he's finally seen enough of this mess and plans to head out.

Except…

He doesn't leave. I can feel him getting nearer and soon enough his big body wraps around me in a hug. It startles me so much that for a second I stop breathing. Alex brings his legs around me and pulls me closer, into his chest, holding me tight. I take a few deep breaths and can feel myself relaxing a bit.

"I know what it's like—that feeling of homesickness," he says, and I close my eyes, letting his deep voice soothe me. "Anna and I were close. We didn't have the greatest parents, they were always more interested in getting drunk than in their children's wellbeing.

"She was five years older than me, and when she graduated high school, she found herself a job and a shitty apartment, and she took me with her. We worked hard to get everything we wanted and all we really had was each other. And that feeling of homesickness—I've felt that every day since she's been gone."

My tears continue to fall freely, thinking about his heartbreak. At least my family is still alive, at least I'll be able to see them someday soon and hug them.

"I'm so sorry," I say, sniffing back more tears.

"Life is unpredictable," he says, voice soft and tickling my ear. "One day you can be fine, and the next you can die because of a brain aneurysm. My point is, you need to take charge of your own life and decide what's most important to you. If seeing your family is important, then *fight* for it," Alex says.

I let my shoulders drop while his arms continue to cage me in. His chin rests on the top of my head and he squeezes his arms around me more. *Good lord, they're so strong.* If he pulls me any closer I'll basically be sitting in his lap.

"We can talk to Nori if you want, I'm sure she'll understand if you miss a few events."

"The last thing I want is to disappoint people," I say, removing one of my hands from the cage he's built around me and placing it on his forearm. The material of his athletic long-sleeve is so soft that I find myself rubbing it back and forth in a soothing motion. He doesn't stop me, so I say, "But you're right. I'll find a workaround. I'll fly my parents in sometime this spring and make up for my missed trip."

"Good. If Jackson tries to intervene, tell me. I know we fight a lot, and I give you a bunch of shit, often for no reason, but..." He takes a deep breath and pulls back enough that I can turn and look at him. "We're in this together, and it's for both our benefit that we make this fake dating arrangement work until the end of your first season."

I nod because he's right. We need to get our shit together and make it look like we're in love. That we want to tear our clothes off each other because we're passionate, not because we want to murder one another.

It's not easy though. Especially since Alex and I are a lot more alike than I realized. We're both stubborn and hotheaded. *And now I know he's just as lonely and homesick as I am.*

"Thank you," I say, slowly standing up and offering him a hand. "I appreciate you confiding in me about Anna."

He nods, his green eyes dampened with sorrow.

"Thanks for listening. And—we've got ourselves a truce," he replies, taking my hand. Alex gives me a long, searching look before he gently lets go and opens the door for me. "Let me give you a ride home."

"I live within walking distance," I say, wiping my face with the bottom of my shirt.

"I'll walk you, then."

SNOWFLAKES FALL PEACEFULLY as we make the short trek to my apartment building, bundled in our jackets and hats.

"Wow, you were not kidding that it's within walking distance," Alex says five minutes later as we reach my building.

"It's not cheap, but the location is great," I say, just to make conversation. I somehow find myself craving his presence. I don't want him to go.

"Yeah, the movie theater is across the street, too. Do you go often?"

"Not really." I grimace. I've actually never been to this theater even though I moved into the apartment in May.

"Too busy?" he asks with a knowing look, and I nod.

I rub my hands together to keep the chill at bay, but instead of heading inside to my apartment, I find myself asking, "Do you want to come in?"

Alex blinks at me, hands deep in his jacket pockets. "I can't—sorry, I have to get back for a team meeting."

"Right, of course." I nod, feeling dumb for even asking. *Just because he showed you a bit of kindness and opened up to you, that doesn't mean he wants to be your friend.*

"But," he says, eyes searching my face, "maybe I can text you one of these days?"

I let out a breath of relief. "Yeah, that would be nice."

"Okay. Are you coming to the game tomorrow night?"

"I'll be there."

Alex grins and pats my head before turning to leave.

"Wait," I say, taking a hold of his jacket.

He takes a step closer to me, keeping the flurries at bay with his massive shoulders. "Yeah?"

"I have a favor to cash in, remember?" I say, bringing back the small favor he owed me from a while ago when we swapped schedules.

His lips are red from the cold and they twitch as he nods. I take a deep breath and ask, "Why did you delete my number?" It's not the question I wanted to ask, but it slips out as I think back on that day and how disappointed I was.

Alex is surprised by the question. He opens his mouth, but nothing comes out for a few seconds. The look on his face tells me everything I need to know. *He regrets it.*

"I was an idiot," he finally says, closing his eyes and sighing deeply. "That day, it wasn't really about you. I had gotten a game suspension for a fight that took place in a pre-season game and I was just—so pissed. I wanted a clean slate this season, I didn't want to be known as the asshole that gets into a fight in every game, and I had already fucked up in the pre-season."

Looking down at me again, he bites his lower lip, shrugging. "Coming back to the arena and finding out that we had to share it felt like a punishment, and I took it out on the wrong person. It wasn't fair, and you didn't deserve it."

I nod, believing him. "So you don't actually hate me and my team?" I ask, needing to hear it.

He laughs but quickly stops when he sees the serious

expression on my face. "Of course I don't. You just—" he says, blowing out a breath and groaning. "You're just so easily riled up, and I like messing with you because you dish out as much as you take."

I contemplate his answer for a moment as I hold his apologetic gaze. "Thank you, for being honest."

Alex nods and turns to actually leave this time.

I take a few steps up to the main door of my building, but then remember—he doesn't have my number anymore.

"Hey!" I yell after him and he turns to face me, continuing to walk backwards. "We need to exchange numbers."

He shakes his head and leaves me with, "No, we don't."

INTERLUDE

How many guesses do I get until you tell me your name?

Three.

Only three? That's harsh, Ashley.

Two left...

Do I get any hints?

No, I want to see what you come up with.

You are one tough cookie, Alana.

Wow, you are one impatient person.

Makes sense, since you stole my Americano :)

One left.

Malia.

There.

That's my last guess.

> You kept my number this whole time?

I did. Did you delete it?

> I did. I'm sorry.

Don't be sorry. I was an asshole.

> Why did you keep it?

Truthfully, that day at the café, I felt something between us. A spark, maybe?

Am I crazy, or did you feel it too?

> You're not crazy.

Are you going to wear my jersey to the game? 😊

> In your dreams. 😊

EIGHT

When I get to the front row seat this time, Josh is already there, two sodas and a large popcorn in his small hands.

I smile and say, "Hey kiddo."

He looks up and quickly stands, giving me a hug. "You came," he says, almost like he can't believe I'm here again.

"Yeah, buddy. Why wouldn't I?"

He steps back and hangs his head, fidgeting with the bottom of his jersey. "You missed the other two games and I thought you were mad at me."

"Why would I be mad at you?" I ask, alarmed. He sits down and I do the same, giving him my full attention. I got here later than expected and the players are already out there, warming up.

"I didn't mean to make fun of you last time. I'm sorry," he says, biting his lip with remorse.

"Kid, there's no way in hell I'd be mad at you for a silly joke. Trust me, I've had my fair share of jabs. I've just been busy, that's all."

"Are you and Cap okay?" he asks and I feel bad for

lying to him about the fake relationship, when Alex is clearly an important presence in this kid's life.

"Oh yeah, everything is great, better than ever," I say enthusiastically, nodding my head up and down.

Josh narrows his eyes at me but relents. "I'm glad you came back. I like having someone to hang out with."

My heart squeezes and I feel bad for not coming back sooner. It's not like I hated watching the game, and I enjoyed the kid's company.

"I'll come more often, at least until my season starts," I promise.

"COME ON, ARE YOU BLIND?" I yell out at the referee that just sent Robbie, one of the Manticores, to the penalty box for tripping with only two minutes left in the game. We lead by two goals, but that's not the point.

Without his cast, Josh is jumping around and flailing his arms in exasperation. I can't help but laugh at his antics and admire the passion he has for the game. This is the kind of energy I want at *my* games too.

Alex is out there on the penalty kill and I'm laser focused on him. He easily meanders between players, getting himself on a breakaway. Josh is on his feet, enraptured by the move too, and when Alex takes the shot, faking it to the right and landing the puck in the top left corner of the net, the whole arena erupts in cheers, my feet involuntarily getting me up and jumping.

They get ready for another face-off but with only ten seconds remaining, the Manticores keep it in their zone and run the clock down. Robbie gets out of the penalty box and the guys from the bench jump over the wall, all of them converging at the home net for a celebration.

Alex winks at me as he skates by us and heads down the tunnel, and I feel a little flutter in my stomach.

"Let's go, we need to get to the other side of the arena."

"For what?" I ask, following Josh up the stairs.

"It's a post-game open skate. Do you not have the calendar for all the activities of the season? There's a lot that we get access to with our season passes."

I laugh and shake my head. Of course there are a lot of perks. But an open skate? "I don't have skates."

"I'm sure you can borrow some, there's always some extra for crew, friends, and family."

"Wow, you really know your way around here."

"I basically live here," Josh says and picks up the pace, making me run after him.

When we reach the other side of the arena, we head down another set of stairs and this time walk over to the tunnel where the Zamboni usually comes out. There's already a line of people here, skates in hand, waiting to sign waivers and head to the makeshift room they set up. Josh grabs my hand and brings us to one of the security guys, who then escorts us to the registration table.

"Josh, hey buddy. Need some skates?" a blond girl wearing a Manticores jacket says.

"Yeah, a pair for Cap's girlfriend too," he says, nodding at me.

My cheeks go red at the mention of Alex and I don't miss the way the girl's eyebrows rise up, perusing me from head to toe. I lift my chin up in defiance and stare her down. Did she expect something else from Cap's *girlfriend*? Is she judging me?

She eventually gives me a smile and looks through all the spare skates they have in a large bin behind the table.

"Have fun, you two," she says cheerfully, handing us the skates. I look down at mine and see she correctly guessed my size. Maybe that's why she was looking me up and down.

I give her a grateful smile and say, "Thanks."

After five minutes of struggling with my laces, I finally feel confident that I won't break my ankle once I hit the ice. They seem snug enough, and Josh is pacing around, waiting for me, so I quickly stand and make my way to him.

"Let's go, let's go. We don't want to miss the players."

"Players?" I ask, confused. But I don't hear Josh reply because I'm too busy hanging on to the door and the small edge of the glass as my feet slide on the ice and I try to balance myself. When I think I've finally got it, I let go of the wall and breathe in and out, arms stretched out in front of me, just in case I slide too much again.

Out of nowhere, I go flying. No—wait, those are arms against my waist and a solid body behind me, lifting me up and spinning us both around so I can face the ice.

Dozens of people are skating around, chatting with players who are coming out of the tunnel, only the bottom half of their equipment still on.

"Put me down, you oaf. You stink," I say, wriggling in Alex's arms. He does as he's told, chuckling in my ear.

"Play nice, Jen and her camera are here," he whispers, hands still on my waist, making sure I don't fall.

"Have you seen my dad?" Josh asks.

"He's grabbing some skates so he can join you," Alex says, nodding to the player's bench where Michael's dark brown hair is visible from where he's bent over.

"Thanks," he says before skating away. *That little traitor ditched me.*

My hands land on top of Alex's and I say, "I think I've got it now."

"What, are you worried I'm gonna get you back? Like how you took me by surprise at the photo-shoot?" Alex bends down to whisper in my ear again and I spin around just in time to see his green eyes sparkle with mischief.

"Oh, hey Jen," he says over my shoulder, and I glare at him. *Bastard.*

"Mind if I snap a few shots?" she says.

Alex grins at me before sweeping me off my feet and into his arms. He hoists me up so that my legs have room to lock at his back. *How in the world does he have this much balance and control on those skates?*

My hands grip the back of his sweaty neck and I make a grossed-out noise. Alex grimaces and says, "Sorry, I didn't think this through. I should have showered first."

I blink down at his face and ignore the snapping of the camera next to us. Did he just...*apologize?* To me?

"It's—fine," I say tentatively. He blinks back at me, also stunned that we're actually being docile towards one another.

"How did it go with your parents? Were they disappointed you couldn't visit?" he asks, voice soft. The question guts me though, and I bite my lip so it doesn't wobble.

I shrug with a sad smile and he nods in understanding. His hands move up and down my back and I realize how warm he is. It's such a huge contrast to the biting cold of the arena that I shiver.

"Where's your jacket?" he asks, his breath soft and warm against my cheek. When did we get so close?

"Somewhere with my shoes." I breathe out.

With a gruff sound, he places me back down, letting me lean on the glass behind me.

"I'll be right back."

I watch him skate to the tunnel and take off at a fast pace. When he turns the corner, I finally take in my surroundings. *What the hell was that?* I've been in his arms before, but did it feel this good then too?

Jen smirks at me from behind her lens and I school my features. If I'm not careful she might capture the real feelings I'm starting to show for the insufferable captain.

She starts to skate up to me but she's distracted, so she doesn't see Michael when he runs into her, sweeping her off her feet. *Literally.* By some miraculous maneuver, he takes the brunt of the fall, Jen landing on top of him, the camera cradled between them. Josh helps her up as they both apologize profusely.

She's usually stoic and witty, always ready with a quip or dry reply. As she stares up at Michael, she seems speechless.

I smile to myself and turn my head just as Alex approaches me with a jersey dangling from his hand. At my confused expression he says, "Don't worry, this one is clean."

Reaching out, I try to grab it from him, but he doesn't let me, putting it on me himself. I look down and laugh when I see I'm drowning in it. The corners of Alex's lips twitch imperceptibly and I flap my arms around in the oversized jersey.

He rolls up the sleeves on both my arms, taking my hand and gently guiding me around the ice. Josh joins us and Jen takes a few more pictures of us before moving on to the rest of the players. I don't miss the way her eyes follow Michael around the ice as she snaps pictures.

Alex signs a few jerseys and hats and before I know it, the night is over, only family and crew left on the ice. My feet are killing me, but I seem to have improved my balance in the last hour.

"Do you want me to walk you home?" Alex asks, escorting me off the ice, making sure I don't fall.

I face him once my feet are safely on the black mat. It still feels...*weird*. Having him on my side instead of against me. I shake my head and give him a smile. "I'll be okay. Oh, I almost forgot the jersey," I say, reaching down to pull it over my head, but Alex's hands stop me.

"Keep it. It's not a game jersey. Besides, it looks good on you."

"Thanks," I say awkwardly, trying to get the flutters in my stomach to die down.

"The gala's in a few days," he says, his focus solely on me and the way I'm fidgeting with the jersey.

"It is. Am I meeting you there?"

"That might be best. I promised Josh I'd spend some time with him, otherwise I would offer to pick you up and ride together."

"Oh, no worries, I'll take a rideshare or something."

"Okay," he says, slowly skating backwards.

"See you tomorrow!" I can't help the smile that overtakes my face thinking about the gala. Jonie and Andrea are going too, and the three of us spent way too much money and time shopping in the last week.

But it's for a good cause. And maybe I want to make a lasting impression on a certain captain.

NINE

The gala is hosted at the most lavish hotel downtown, the Harmony Plaza. Jonie, Andrea, and I take our time walking through the marble-floored lobby, following the line of people in gowns and tuxedos headed into the Grand Ballroom. My eyes roam over the multiple decorations around the arch to the ballroom—wreaths, bells, and giant bows on each pillar. Inside, past the check-in table and the people mingling, I spot a giant Christmas tree in the middle of the room, dressed in nothing but thousands of little twinkling lights and gold ribbon.

"Names?" the young woman at the table asks once we approach.

"Malia Kahale," I say, taking off my long beige coat as my friends move down the line to check in.

"Ah, yes. Our beloved Thunderbird captain. Welcome," she says with a warm smile, and I think I recognize her from the post-game open skate event.

"Thanks," I say, taking in a shaky breath, trying to let the nervous energy out. A volunteer hands me a ticket and holds out his arm expectantly. It takes me a moment longer than it should for me to realize he's waiting for my coat.

I blush and hand it over, holding on to my clutch with one hand and smoothing over my silky black dress with the other. I debate waiting around for Alex, but I don't know when he's getting here. Or if he's already inside. I almost want to text him, but that's a dangerous thought.

"We're going to find a bathroom," Jonie says, swaying her hips in a dark green dress that fits her like a glove.

"Want to come with?" Andrea asks, her dark blond hair pinned up to display the high-collared gown she got in a baby blue color.

"I'll mingle and catch you later."

"Since when do you mingle?" Jonie asks.

"Please, she's looking for her *boyfriend*."

"You guys are impossible," I say, leaving them chuckling behind.

Walking through the room, I have to admit, the organizers did a fantastic job. Servers are walking around with various hors d'oeuvres that look and smell incredible. Someone offers me a mimosa with rosemary sprigs and cranberries. I take it gingerly and nod at the bright-eyed guy, who gives me a wink.

Maybe a few big gulps will help with my nerves. The fizzy drink is sweet and delicious as it hits my tongue, and I close my eyes and sigh contentedly. If nothing else good comes out of tonight as we try and get people to donate to our chosen non-profits and buy season tickets, at least the drinks and food are delectable.

"There you are."

My eyes fly open and I spin on my heels to face the man who's been invading not just my dreams lately, but my day-to-day thoughts. And he looks *fucking incredible*. The forest green suit is perfectly tailored to his body, and even in my four-inch heels, he still towers over me, his green eyes bright, piercing, and trailing down the front of my body.

Selfishly, I want his eyes on me, so I don't dare move a muscle. Alex's eyes roam over my plunging v-neck but they don't linger there long. Instead, his gaze trails down, down, down to the slit in my silk dress that exposes most of my left leg and thigh.

His eyes flare and I spot the moment his fists clench at his side. *What would his hands feel like on me? Under my dress, lifting it higher and higher and—*

"You clean up nice," he says, clearing his throat. "For a second there, I thought you'd show up in your leggings," he continues, smirking down at me. "Or better yet—my jersey."

I huff but find that I'm not as bothered by his teasing anymore. *Huh, when did that happen?* Maybe it's the mimosa, or the fact that he's here with me, that makes me relax more.

"You don't look so bad yourself. I see you've left the backwards hat at home for once."

Alex smiles a full, unabashed smile, teeth on display and a dimple popping in his right cheek. I bite my lip at the sight of it, trying to keep my composure, but *shit*. How am I supposed to ignore the flutters in my stomach now?

That boyish look in combination with his strong body and pillowy lips make him irresistible.

"Ready to pretend you like me?"

I frown at the words and Alex's eyes search my face. *Right, Malia, this is pretend.* I muster up a smile and nod, finishing off my mimosa and placing the empty glass on a nearby cocktail table.

"I am now. Do we even know what we need to do?"

"Talk to some of the guests, really sell them on the team

and how great this season is going to be," Alex says, holding out his arm for me.

I take it reluctantly, and just when I think I see a hint of hesitation in his perfectly schooled expression, he leans in and whispers, "Don't worry, I won't bite, sweetheart. Not tonight."

A shiver runs through me, and I can't stop it in time. Alex's smirk comes back in full swing, and the bastard even winks at me. *He winks.*

I will my legs to move and follow him, even though all they want is to turn to jelly.

I ZONE OUT and deflate a little more as another rich person decides to place his focus solely on Alex tonight. It's like I don't even exist, even though I've been attached to his arm for the past hour, being paraded around the room.

On one hand, I'm glad, because I hate talking to strangers, especially when I'm the center of attention. On the other hand, I feel like they *should* be asking me questions too, because this fundraiser is for my team as well. *I should be doing more.*

My stomach lets out a small rumble and Alex looks down at me with a questioning look on his face. I smile tightly and try to listen to the third—no, fourth—old white guy talking about the Calder Cup with an intense passion.

"So Melia." The old man grabs my attention, mispronouncing my name as Mel-ee-yah instead of Muh-lee-ah. "What will you be bringing to the community?"

My mouth opens but nothing comes out. *Fuck.* I've practiced a bunch of PR answers, I've been vetted by Nori, but now when it counts, I don't know what to say. So I wing it. "Well, um—volleyball, that's not something the city has had before. A team, I mean—a professional team."

The man—Richard, I think his name is—looks at me, wholly unimpressed by my half-assed, mumbled answer. I swallow down the disappointment in myself and grab another mimosa from a nearby server, pulling Alex's arm with me.

I take an anxious sip of it as the men around me go quiet. Then Alex pipes up, "Richard, didn't you say you had a daughter?"

"I do," he says, straightening up and looking proud. "She's just been accepted to University of Michigan. She'll be starting there next fall."

"That's amazing, congratulations," Alex says, and his arm lets go of me to grab my hand instead, squeezing it. I look up at him, confused, and he widens his eyes at me to jump into the conversation.

"That's fantastic," I say, a little too enthusiastically. "What will she be studying?"

"Well, she's still deciding, but she got in on an athletic scholarship. She'll be playing volleyball."

Oh. Oh, I really should be doing better, because this is the right guy to try and convince to donate or purchase courtside season tickets. Except I'm *really* bad at this. I don't know how to sell myself.

"You know, the Thunderbirds are currently one of the most talked about professional teams in volleyball. They have a lot of great talent—players recruited from all over the country, even University of Michigan. Right, sweetheart?" Alex says, turning to me again.

I stare at him open mouthed. He talks about my team

like he actually keeps up with us. The corners of his lips twitch, and I close my mouth with a snap.

"That's right, *honey*," I respond, and squeeze his hand.

"Oh, well, I didn't know that," Richard says, frowning.

"Maybe your daughter could benefit from sitting courtside this season?" Alex supplies, letting the question trail off.

"That's a great idea, babe," I chip in. "She would be seeing professionals play up close, maybe even gain a mentor or network with an alumna from her future university?"

Richard's face brightens for the first time since we started this conversation, and I relax a little more. "Yes, I think that's a fantastic idea. Can you make this happen?" Richard asks.

"Absolutely, I will personally see to it," I say.

"Well, thank you, Melia," he says, nodding to me.

"It's Malia," Alex says, sounding my name out for him. The flutter in my stomach is back and I stroke the back of his thumb gratefully.

"Right, my apologies," Richard says before taking his leave.

"Good job," Alex says, beaming at me.

I can't help but smile back. "Thank you, I appreciate the help."

"Nah, it was just a nudge." He shrugs, still holding my hand. We both look down at it at the same time and I expect him to let it go. I expect *me* to let it go. But we stay like that, fingers intertwined, until my stomach rumbles again.

"Let's get some food," Alex says, leading me to the extravagant buffet table.

THE ENTIRE TABLE falls silent as Alex and I approach with our plates stacked high. There are three of my teammates interspersed throughout other Manticores players, all of them mingling and having a good time.

They look at us expectantly as we take our seats, and I finally ask, "What?"

Everyone shares this incredulous look, and Jonie finally says, "Glad to see your 'relationship' has made you both act civil with one another." I roll my eyes at them and dig into my food, mouth watering.

"Yeah, what happened to you two being sworn enemies? How did you go from that to 'dating'?" one of the hockey players pipes up.

"Settle down, Robbie," Alex chides him, but when I lift my head, I see a small smile playing on his lips.

The night continues with more chatter and pleasantries, until the organizer announces the auction is about to start.

"What are they auctioning—?" I stop, blinking hard at the sight in front of me. The four hockey players at my table are all standing up, shrugging their suit jackets off and rolling up their sleeves. It's not just me affected by the picture—my girls are also staring open-mouthed.

"Please welcome to the stage, four of our Manticores: Jordan Hill, Robbie Elliot, Trip Dasher, and their beloved captain, Alex Dionis," the emcee announces, and everyone in the room starts cheering.

As they head to the stage, Alex stops behind me and leans in to whisper something. "Thinking about bidding on me, sweetheart?"

If there was any room in my heels for my toes to curl, they would. *Fuck*, why is it that every little thing he does lately turns me on?

Alex winks like he can read my thoughts and makes his way to the stage. I'm left flustered and blushing at the table, trying to hide it with a few more sips of mimosa.

"We'll start the bidding with Jordan Hill, one of our top defensemen. Jordan is a night owl; he enjoys playing video games late into the night. His favorite music genres are folk and indie, and he enjoys winter sports. Our bidding starts at two hundred dollars for an ice-skating lesson with Jordan."

Paddles start flying up and the bidding quadruples in under a minute as my teammates and I look around, stupefied. How did we not know this was a thing? Are they planning to do the same with us?

"Sold for twelve hundred dollars!"

"Wow, this is..." Jonie trails off.

"Fucking cool," Andrea supplies.

"Language, this is a classy event," I chide, taking another mouthful of the cranberry chicken dish in front of me as they roll their eyes at me fondly.

"A tour of the arena with Trip Dasher, sold for nine hundred and fifty dollars!"

My eyes dart to Alex, and I wonder if they're saving him to be auctioned off last. Like he can sense my thoughts and lingering looks, his gaze finds mine. His posture is casual, hands in his pockets, those damn rolled-up sleeves displaying his tattooed arms. Alex flexes them as my gaze trails down and I snap my eyes to his again. The bastard smirks at me, eyes lighting up with mischief. *He must know the effect he has on me.*

"Next up, we have hockey center Robbie Elliot. In his spare time, Robbie loves cooking, playing with his cats, and hosting game nights with his friends. His biggest dream outside of hockey is to one day give back to the community that helped shape him into the man he is today. The bid will start at two hundred for a private cooking lesson with Robbie at his family's establishment, The Arcadian."

Paddles are going up left and right again and Alex is still smirking at me. *I wonder...*

My fingers reach for the paddle that sits on the table, and I inhale deeply. I only spare Alex a glance before my hand grips the handle and flies up.

"Three hundred dollars from the Thunderbirds captain. Uh-oh, do we have some trouble in paradise? Do I hear three twenty-five?"

Alex's smirk is gone in an instant as he turns his full attention to Robbie, staring daggers at the back of the poor guy's head. I bite the inside of my cheek to keep my smile from taking over.

Seems like he might be jealous.

"Four hundred!" a woman with dark red hair exclaims.

"Four twenty-five" I say, my hand moving quickly. *Fuck*, I need to stop. There's no way I could spend that much, and besides, I'm not even interested in Robbie like that. But the look on Alex's face is worth it. Jaw clenched, muscles in his forearms tight, he looks the picture-perfect jealous boyfriend.

Robbie's eyes widen when he hears my bid again and he falters where he bounces on his feet. When he looks back at Alex, he shrugs a little in the face of his ire, conveying that he has no idea what I'm up to.

"Damn girl, you're really going for it, huh?" Jonie says, and I drop the paddle to the table, cheeks red from embarrassment.

"No. Shut up."

"Five hundred, do we have five twenty-five?" the emcee says.

"No, no, I'm all for you making your fake boyfriend jealous." Andrea smirks and wiggles her eyebrows at me.

"Would you keep it down? No one else besides you knows it's fake," I whisper, placing my head in my hands and trying to tune out the rest of the auction.

Okay, things I've learned tonight.

1. Alex knows more about volleyball than he claims to and actually helped me out tonight.

2. He's been kind and thoughtful lately, and I've started to really like that side of him.

3. When I try and bid on his friend for a date, he feels jealous.

4. I really, really want him.

"And last but not least, we've got Alex Dionis, the Manticores captain. The bidding for a platonic date with the captain starts at five hundred dollars. The captain asked us to specify it would be platonic as he's currently dating the lovely Miss Malia." I choke and sputter, my head lifting up to Alex.

If looks could kill, I would be dead and buried six feet under right about now. Alex is *glowering* at me and now I actually feel bad for putting that look on his face when earlier tonight I'd gotten him to smile at me. And he turned the auction date into a platonic one to keep up appearances.

"I'm sorry," I mouth to him and notice the deep inhale he takes by the movement of his shoulders. Alex looks away from me and my stomach sinks. *No, this is wrong.*

I will him to look my way again with my thoughts alone, but he won't budge, keeping his gaze fixed straight ahead.

Please, look at me again.

"Seven fifty, do we have seven seventy-five?" the emcee asks, and my hand raises without a second thought.

"Eight hundred!" I all but yell out.

"The Thunderbird captain strikes again. Maybe this date will not be platonic after all."

"Eight fifty," someone says from the table behind me, and I whip around to glare at the woman. She looks to be about sixty and at first glance you'd think she'd be a sweet old lady, but I don't like the wicked gleam in her eyes as she takes in Alex.

Don't be dumb, Malia. You can't afford this.

Ah, fuck it.

"One thousand!" I say, reveling in the way Alex is looking at me now. The smile he gives me is softer than any I've seen on him, and it stupidly makes me think it's reserved for me alone.

"Fifteen hundred," the woman behind me pipes up again, and I blanch.

Fuck, I definitely can't pay that much.

I look nervously between her and Alex, but he gives me a head shake. He doesn't want me to continue. I breathe a sigh of relief and place the paddle under my butt so I'm not tempted to raise it again, even as a tight knot of jealousy coils in my stomach as I listen to the rest of the auction. *Are you really that surprised he's sought after? He's clearly the hottest guy here.*

"Sold for thirty-five hundred dollars! Thank you everyone for participating in the live auction. The remaining items and memorabilia will be auctioned off via the mobile application. If you need assistance setting up an account, you can find us at the volunteer table."

The guys come back and resume their places at the table, and for a moment no one says anything.

"That was so wild. Do you guys get auctioned off like this every year?" Andrea asks, leaning in on her elbows.

"They rotate which players get to participate, but pretty much," Jordan says.

"Why didn't we get auctioned off?" Jonie asks with a frown.

"Because you're nobody. Yet..." Andrea says with a big smile.

Alex's large hand lands on the back of my neck and I—I stop listening, I stop *breathing*. I'm solely focused on the spot below my ear where he's tracing his thumb back and forth.

Leaning in, he says, "Care to join me for a dance?"

ALEX LEADS me to the dance floor, where a violin rendition of "The Night We Met" is playing. The hand that's holding mine doesn't let go as he spins in place to face me. Instead, he brings it up, leading me through the dance. His other hand lands on my waist and I rest mine on his shoulder, my thumb tracing the outline of his collarbone through his shirt.

He doesn't say anything about my bidding shenanigans earlier, and part of me is disappointed. Alex does, however, keep his eyes focused on me throughout the whole dance, and his expression is more open than I've ever seen it. He's unguarded, and it makes the butterflies in my stomach come back in full flutter.

We move so effortlessly together, so completely in sync, and I wonder what else we'd be good at together.

"Did you have fun tonight?" he asks, voice low and deep as he pulls in closer, his nose brushing my forehead.

"I did," I say a little breathlessly, tilting my head to meet his eyes again. I could get lost in those mossy green eyes.

I could so easily fall for him.

Alex looks over my shoulder at someone and as he spins us around in our slow dance, I see Jen with her camera pointed at us once more.

"Do I have your permission to kiss you?" he asks, voice catching at the end.

I can't help the sad smile that takes over my face. *I want him to kiss me for real, not because of a camera.*

"You don't have to ask every time," I mumble. "If there's a camera around, just go for it."

He searches my eyes for a moment, frowning. I pull my hand from his and wind both my arms around his neck, guiding him closer to me. I still need to reach up on my toes to meet his face, but Alex's hands on my lower back help steady me.

This kiss is nothing like the one at the ice-skating rink. There's nothing tentative about the press of his lips against mine, but it also lacks the intensity of our last kiss.

Alex's lips move against mine languidly and I'm fighting between the desire to open myself up to it because his lips are so soft and warm against mine, and I can taste the orange from the mimosa he was drinking, and to shut it down, because *it isn't real.*

He's kissing me out of some misplaced duty to our fake dating arrangement, not because he actually wants me. *But fuck, I want him.*

Just thinking about it makes my chest hurt and I pull back from the kiss, trying to tamp down the emotion that threatens to overtake me.

"Was kissing me that bad?" Alex whispers as I blink back tears. "Hey, what's wrong?" he asks, concern taking over his features, his hand reaching out to touch my face.

"Nothing," I say with a tight smile, avoiding his eyes and taking a step back. "I need to find a restroom."

I leave him there, in the middle of the dance floor, his hand in midair, still reaching for me, and I try not to break out in a run.

The bathroom is blessedly empty, so I can throw my pity party for one in peace. Going up to the large vanity, hands gripping the edge, I take in my appearance in the mirror. My lips are puffy, my lipstick smudged, and I grab a tissue to try and fix it without smearing it off.

A couple tears fall, and I do my best to wipe them away without messing up my mascara.

I take in a few deep breaths, trying to calm my nerves, but Alex's words swirl around in my brain. *Was kissing me that bad?*

I should have been honest at the moment. *No, kissing you was amazing, I just wish it was real.*

Tossing the balled-up tissues in the trash, I force myself to let this go and enjoy the rest of the night. When I open the door and exit the bathroom, I stop in my tracks.

Alex is leaning against the wall, eyes closed tight, his hand running through his hair, tugging at the roots. His suit jacket is back on and he looks devastatingly beautiful. I bite my quivering lip and take a few steps towards him, keeping enough of a distance that I don't do something stupid like reach out for him.

At the sound of my heels against the marble floor, his eyes snap open and latch on to me. What I find there is a mixture of regret and concern. *For me.* And I hate myself for making him feel like he did anything wrong. I swallow hard and approach him, hugging my arms around myself, fighting off more than just the chill of the hallway.

Alex's eyes dart to the movement and he quickly takes off his jacket, only hesitating for a second before stepping up to me and swinging it around my shoulders. I grab it and pull it tighter around me, cocooning myself in his warmth and fresh smell of birch. The woodsy, leathery smell makes me relax enough that I look up and meet his eyes.

"Why did you run away?" he asks, his warm eyes watching my every move.

I contemplate lying, but what's the point anymore? *Just tell him how you feel.*

When I'm still quiet, he resumes tugging at his hair in distress. "I'm sorry. I shouldn't have suggested the kiss. You're clearly not comfortable with it, and I should have just dropped it."

Not comfortable? No, that's not it at all. I start shaking my head, but he goes on.

"I did the same thing at the ice-skating event, and you ran away then too. Fuck, *Malia*, I'm so sorry."

"*Alex,* stop," I say, reaching out and grabbing his hand, stopping his pacing.

He swallows and looks down at our hands, where I'm rubbing his thumb in a soothing motion.

"You didn't do anything wrong," I say, taking a deep breath. "I'm not upset because you kissed me."

"Then why?" he asks, a small frown taking over his features.

I sigh and squeeze his hand, keeping my gaze on the contact there. "I just wish you'd kiss me for real. Not just in front of a camera," I say quietly.

Alex is quiet for a moment and my tears come back in full force, the lump in my throat making it hard to swallow or add anything more to my confession. But then his free hand comes up and lifts my chin up.

His face is blurry but his smile is impossible to miss. It's the soft one he gave me earlier, the small dimple making a reappearance and making him look soft and boyish. *I want to kiss that spot. I want him to be mine.*

"You do?" Alex asks, his warm breath tickling my lips.

I nod and subconsciously lean in further. But he doesn't kiss me right away. He steadies me with another hand on my waist and says, "Then tell me something. Why did you bid on Robbie?"

I groan and drop my head to his chest, fisting the side of his shirt. "Because I'm an idiot. I wanted to—" I stop, biting my lip and looking back up at him. His eyebrows are raised and he's genuinely curious. Does he not get that I was trying to make him jealous?

Sighing, I admit, "I wanted to draw a reaction from you."

He nods in understanding and says, "And? What did you find out?"

"Maybe you're a little bit jealous."

Alex snorts and it's my turn to raise my eyebrows. "Sweetheart, I was ready to push my own friend and teammate off the stage because I thought you wanted to go on a date with him. I was more than jealous," he admits softly, his hand returning to my face, thumb rubbing my bottom lip back and forth.

"Oh."

"Yeah, oh," he agrees, and walks us backwards until my back meets the wall. After a moment he says, "Can I kiss you?"

"I thought we already went over this. You don't have to

ask," I say, heart in my throat because *holy shit*, he actually feels the same way.

Shaking his head, he says, "There's no cameras this time. And I want to make sure it's what you really want."

"I've wanted it—*you*—for a while now."

Alex grins and drops his head in the crook of my neck, peppering me with kisses from the spot below my ear, to my jaw, and cheeks. It's so sweet and so completely unlike him that I can't help but giggle. He swallows the sound down when his lips meet mine with such fervor, I'd be knocked back a step if I wasn't already leaning on the wall.

We move to the choreography of our own bodies, so in sync that I don't even know where he ends and where I begin. We're just a tangle of limbs, my hands not being able to decide whether they want to stay in his hair, mussing it further, or if they want to roam over his strong back. So I do a combination of both, which probably looks like I'm trying to maul him, my fingertips digging into his shoulder as his tongue plunges into my mouth, tangling with my own.

One of his hands never leaves my face, tilting my head this way and that, taking the kiss deeper and making me breathlessly pant for him each time he pulls back. The other hand moves from my waist to the slit in my dress, gripping my thigh and bringing my leg up and around his waist.

The move pushes us even closer together and I can feel the hardness of his cock against my stomach. I moan into the kiss and he lets out a ragged breath, resting his forehead against mine. I swear I can feel him twitching against me and I involuntarily rock my hips against him. His grip on me tightens as he says, "You look incredible in this dress. It's driving me fucking crazy."

A whine spills from my lips and Alex kisses me again, a

softer, shorter peck against my lips, but I feel the intensity of it down to my core.

I need more.

"What are you going to do about it?" I rasp out against his mouth.

He pulls back, pupils expanded. I follow the movement of his tongue as he licks his lips, and I can't help but picture this same expression on his face while he's between my legs. My cheeks flush and he grins, like he knows exactly where my filthy mind just went.

"Want to get out of here?" he asks.

I answer with a nod and another kiss, biting his plump bottom lip.

"Take me home," I say.

TEN

The car ride to Alex's apartment is more charged than anything I've ever experienced. I keep looking over at him, making sure this is real. That this is actually happening and it's not just my wild imagination. Every time I do, he returns the look, his gaze molten, fingers twitching on the steering wheel in anticipation of touching me.

I squirm in the seat in an attempt to relieve some of the pressure between my legs. Alex's hand reaches out and grips my thigh over the silky material of my dress, his thumb finding a patch of skin at the slit and rubbing at the spot. My hand covers his and I want to move his touch to where I need him the most, but I'm not going to endanger us while he's driving.

So instead, I hold his hand and admire the way his fingers splay out, covering two-thirds of my leg. I trace the prominent veins on the back of his hand as he flexes his fingers, digging harder into my thigh. I'm so incredibly turned on that I don't even care if he leaves bruises along the way.

I hope he does.

I want him so badly, but it's not just the physical aspect. I want the intimacy, and the connection too, and while we were in sync earlier tonight, a little seed of doubt creeps in.

What if he just wants sex? Would I turn it down if that was the case? Or would I demand more?

The car comes to a stop in front of a tall building at the edge of downtown, across from the farmer's market. I've been to the area before, but didn't realize this was an apartment complex.

"Here we are," he says with one last squeeze to my thigh, before he gets out of the car. I put my arms through the sleeves of my coat and Alex opens the door for me, holding one hand out to help me.

I take it and carefully step out onto the slick road. The recent snow and ice we got is not helpful in my four-inch heels, and my feet slide out from under me with my first step. Alex catches me easily and holds me to him while he closes the door and locks the car. Then, in one sweep, he bends down and picks me up, one arm under my knees and one across my back, carrying me to the door bridal style.

I lock my arms together around his neck and breathe in his woodsy smell, hiding a smile in the face of his gallantry. He doesn't set me down right away, but carries me all the way to the elevator.

"I guess chivalry isn't dead after all," I say when my feet touch the ground.

The elevator doors open and we step in at the same time. Perfectly in sync. Alex pushes the button for the fifth floor and turns to me. He smirks and winks at me, pulling me into him once more. I reach out and trace the sharp lines of his jaw with both hands, kissing my way down the column of his throat to the hollow spot below. His chest rises and falls rapidly and I place one hand over his heart, finding it beating hard.

"Nervous, *Cap*?" I ask, watching him swallow and let out a harsh breath.

"I don't want to fuck this up," he says, cupping the back of my head and bringing me into a hug. I feel all my earlier doubts dissipate as I realize that this means just as much to him as it does to me.

"You won't," I say, but the sound is muffled by his coat and the erratic beat of our hearts.

The elevator dings and we walk hand in hand to the door of his apartment. He presses his palm against the biometric lock and opens the door. Looking at me over his shoulder, Alex leads me into his home.

We don't make it further than the entryway before he's spinning around, pinning me against the door, his palms flat against it, caging me in. I should be alarmed at how fast things are moving, but instead there's a strange calmness that overtakes me.

Like I'm right where I'm supposed to be.

Biting my lip, I reach up and take one of Alex's hands, guiding it back to the slit in my dress. He caresses the flesh there, eyes focused entirely on my face, a small smirk playing at his lips. Leaning in, he places a chaste kiss on my cheek and lifts my leg up, trying to get us back in the same position from the gala.

Except both our coats are in the way, too many layers and not enough contact. I let out a whimper, tugging at his hair, *needing him* like my life depends on it. My brain says I shouldn't have these feelings again, that this attachment came too quickly, but all I want at this moment is *him*.

Unguarded, unfiltered, and utterly naked.

"Coats off," I beg him, my teeth scraping his jaw, before pressing a kiss to the same spot.

Alex's breathing is ragged and his eyes reflect so much longing right before he kisses me. *No, he devours me.* His hands move reverently over my body— soft touches to my waist, up my sides, over my collarbone before he slowly peels off my coat, his fingertips skimming over my shoulders and down my arms, letting the garment drop to the floor.

I want to do the same with him, but I'm rooted to the spot. This is *too much*. He's taking me in like I'm something worth worshiping, like there's no other place he'd rather be, no one he'd rather do this with.

With a step back, he takes off his own coat, dropping it on top of mine. When he reaches out for me again, I say, "Wait."

He immediately stops and blinks out of his lust. *Fuck, that's not what I want.* His mouth opens to ask me what's wrong, but I don't let him say anything further. With more confidence than I've ever had in my body, I say, "Take off all your clothes."

Alex looks stunned for a moment, but a slow smile stretches his perfect mouth and he slowly takes off his suit jacket, moving to the buttons of his shirt, his eyes on me the whole time he pops them open.

This is torture and I must be a masochist. Because as much as I want him to fuck me against this door; I want to savor him. Every single part— from his long, deft fingers, to the veins in his forearm and his tattoos, to his broad chest that's heaving, to his abs and the trail of black hair below.

He stops, his hand hovering over the button at his pants, looking at me with such an intensity that I want to drop to my knees and peel the rest of his clothes off myself. But I think I quite like having this control over him, telling him what to do. So I mirror his smirk from earlier and say, "I said take off *all* your clothes."

Alex's fingers twitch like he'd like nothing better than to grab me and punish me for my insolence, but he follows my command, a muscle in his cheek pulsing with the clench of his jaw. My smirk gets wiped off the moment he unzips his pants and swiftly takes off both his slacks and his boxers.

Fuck, I did not think this through. I've thought about him naked plenty of times, in my shower, at the gym, in my bed at night. But I never thought I'd get to see him in real life. *And he is a masterpiece.*

His cock is thick and long, erect against him. A bead of precum leaks out and I watch it in fascination as it rolls down the vein of his cock. My mouth waters and I swallow, still staring. *Maybe say something. Stop staring at his massive fucking cock for a second and meet his eyes.* But I can't. I'm picturing all the ways he can ruin me, and how good he'd feel inside me, filling me up.

Alex moves and it jostles me out of my daydream. He takes off his socks and takes a step closer to me, ready to do whatever I tell him to. I'm getting braver. Or maybe stupider. Because instead of telling him to fuck me, I say, "Touch yourself."

He makes a noise that sounds close to choking and when I finally look up at his face, I see that he's blushing. He's blushing so hard that it deepens and spreads down his neck and over his chest. I bite my lip in the face of his reaction and encourage him further. "I'll let you touch me after."

His response is immediate, his right hand fisting his cock and giving his head a tug. The movement is accompanied by one of the sexiest moans I've ever heard in my life as he drops his head back.

"Fuck, yes," I whisper. All the muscles in his body are tight, but I'm too focused on the moans he lets out. They're breathy and needy and I wonder what other sounds I can draw out from him.

"Come closer," I rasp out, leaning on the door behind me, finding the need to steady my shaky legs.

Alex does as he's told, breathing hard, chest heaving as he continues to stroke himself for me. He's so close now that I'm once again surrounded by his signature smell, feeling dizzy from how intoxicating he is. His touch is a needle, expertly tattooing himself under my skin in such a way that I will never be able to get him out.

Our breaths mingle as he leans in, but I choose to torture us both further. I gently reach out and place a hand over his, mid-stroke. I bring it up to my mouth and lick two of his fingers before taking them in my mouth and sucking hard, letting them go with a pop.

Alex exhales sharply against me and falls forward, catching himself with a palm on the door at the last second. His mouth finds the spot where my neck and shoulder meet and he breathes out. "Can I please touch you? Put my mouth on you?"

"Do you think you deserve to?"

"No," he says, tongue darting out to lick at the spot. "But I want to anyway."

I let out a shaky breath and bring his still glistening fingers to my breast, pressing his palm against it. Alex groans and presses into me, his painfully hard cock meeting my hip bone as his hand frees my breast from my dress, fingers pinching the hard, sensitive bud.

Moaning, I tip my head back against the door and he takes it as the invitation it is to devour my neck. He alternates between licks and sucks and gentle kisses, driving me wild with desire.

When I reach down and grasp his cock in my much smaller hand, he pulls back quickly. "I'm too close. I don't want to ruin your dress," he says, pressing a kiss to the corner of my mouth.

"Then take it off."

"I have a better idea." He smiles and drops down to his knees in front of me. If I wasn't already leaning on the door, I would have staggered in shock. Because the sight of Alex on his knees in front of me is not one I'll ever forget. His black hair is messy, sticking out in all directions, and I let myself reach out and thread my fingers through it, gently scraping my short nails against his scalp.

Alex groans and grabs the back of my thighs, hands kneading, fingers digging in, moving up and down in the same pattern. He trails a hand down to my left calf and caresses it sweetly before lifting my leg up over his shoulder and nipping at my thigh.

"Thought you said you wouldn't bite." I breathe out in a lusty daze, feeling the smile he's hiding against my skin.

In a second, he's going to find out how utterly drenched I am for him. In a second, his mouth is going to be on *me*.

I don't have time to be self-conscious or worry about it because Alex is lifting up my dress, bunching it at my waist and taking one of my hands from his hair and pressing it to the fabric, making me hold it in place.

His nose grazes my mound and it's my turn to let out a loud moan. He curses softly and presses a kiss there, dragging his tongue over my already-soaked lacy underwear.

"Fuck, you're so wet for me, sweetheart."

"Please," I say, not knowing what it is I need from him.

If it's his mouth, his fingers, or his cock. But something, anything, before I die of horniness.

Alex pulls back, letting my leg drop back to the floor, and just when I think that maybe he's changed his mind, he uses both hands to drag my underwear down my legs, throwing it on top of his pile of clothes.

The sight of the black lace landing there with a thud amongst his suit is so filthy that I pull at his hair, snapping his head back to meet my eyes.

"You've made such a mess of me. You better clean it all up."

Eyes sparkling, Alex grins up at me, throwing one leg over his shoulder, then the other. Before I know it, he's standing up, lifting me up higher against the door, his head between my legs.

I squeal and lock my feet together at his back. I'm leaning against the door, my ass hovering in the air as Alex holds me there, one hand on my waist, the other on my back. I don't have time to worry about the position or if he'll drop me because his mouth is on me, and I lose all my thoughts.

His tongue is hot and eager against my sensitive bud as he flicks it slowly, then picks up the pace. My hands scramble against the door, trying to find some purchase with no luck.

Pulling back, he says, "Hold onto my hair. Do that thing again where you scratch your nails."

"Fuck," I say, delving into his soft locks, scratching his scalp with one hand and tugging at the root with the other.

Alex moans against my clit and I feel the vibration of it all the way down to my toes. "You taste so sweet," he says, tongue trailing up and down my slit, dipping inside me. I clench my legs around his head and tug harder, unable to stop myself.

The coil in my stomach is so tight and I'm so, so fucking close. "More, please. Make me come with your wicked tongue."

"Hm, now you like my wicked tongue?" he says, one hand trailing down from my ass cheek to my pussy, and I let out more embarrassing moans.

One of his fingers, the middle one, dips inside me and I try to move against his mouth, searching for the friction I need. The grinding movement startles him and he brings both hands back to my waist, making sure I don't fall.

Breathing hard against me, he says, "Fuck, don't scare me like that."

"Sorry," I mumble incoherently, only half meaning it. He laughs and pulls back from the door with me still in his arms. I yelp, but he shushes me and carefully steps over the pile of clothes, carrying me to the couch.

It's dark in here, but the blinds are open and the moonlight filters in, giving me glimpses of a minimalistic living room, with a large sectional and a TV in the corner of the room.

Alex easily places me down on the couch, kneeling in front of me. For a second we are frozen, taking in each other's appearance. He's deliciously disheveled and his lips are coated in my wetness and *fuck* if that's not the hottest thing.

My dress is pulled down, exposing a nipple, and the rest of it is bunched around my waist. I sit up and pull the whole thing over my head, letting it drop to the floor. Alex leans down and captures my lips in a kiss. This one is slow, meticulous even, as he swirls his tongue around mine, catching my bottom lip with his teeth and tugging.

"Is this a dream?" he asks in a low voice, almost not believing that I'm real. Earlier tonight, I felt the same way.

"If it is, I don't want to wake up," I say, cupping his jaw and planting my lips on his.

It doesn't take us long to get back the intensity we found before. Alex presses me into the couch, pinning my legs with his large hands, spreading me open for him to feast on. He teases me mercilessly with his tongue, learning my reactions and pulling back at the last second.

He has me panting and writhing under his mouth and I say, "I think I still hate you a little bit."

Alex chuckles darkly and scrapes his teeth on my sensitive bud, making me buck up against him. He lets go of one of my legs and pumps a single finger inside me. The unexpected move has me clenching around him and I dig my heel into his shoulder.

"So, so close," I say, hands fisting the pillows I found on the couch. He gives me what I want, finally letting me come. He adds a second finger, then a third, pumping in and out to the same staccato of his tongue. And when he curls his fingers, finding that perfect spot inside me, I explode in a flurry of moans and curses, white spots enveloping my vision.

I've never felt anything like this in my whole life and I think I might have actually died from the intense orgasm. Except my heart is still beating, quite erratically, and my body is still moving, toes curling, fingers twitching in Alex's hair. *When did they get there?*

And Alex—I prop myself up on my elbows, looking down at the man who just made me see stars. His fingers are still inside me, waiting for me to stop pulsing around him, his thumb tracing featherlight touches on my clit, making me spasm, and his head is resting on my stomach, taking deep breaths.

"Are you okay?" I ask, wondering why he's not already lying next to me, asking me to reciprocate.

Lifting his eyes to me, he gives me a pained look. He looks stunning, the edges of his jaw more sharp in the moonlight, the strain of his muscles emphasizing his beautiful body, his green eyes taken up by so much black. But it's that pained look that startles me into motion, sitting up fully and wrapping my arms around his neck.

"What's wrong?"

He laughs and shakes his head. "Fuck, nothing is wrong. I'm trying to hold myself together."

"Why?"

"Because—" He falters, squeezing his eyes shut. "I don't want you to be disappointed. And at the rate we're going, I might come in two seconds flat."

I laugh, kissing him deeply, raking my nails across his scalp again, just like I know he likes now. "I don't care about any of that. But I do want you to feel just as good as I did."

Another kiss, another tug of his hair. "Come here," I say, not recognizing my own voice as it comes out sultry and hardened by need.

Alex climbs on the couch next to me and I steal another kiss before I reach down and pump him. He's hard and hot in my hand and I rub my thumb over the vein that runs from the base of his cock to the head. He twitches and swears, letting his head rest all the way back, exposing the strong column of his throat.

I straddle him, with enough space to continue to pump him, relishing in the sounds of his moans and the grip of his hand on my waist. I press myself more against him, sucking at a particular spot on his neck and rubbing my thumb over the slit, coating the wetness around.

"*Malia.*" When he whispers my name with such need, I pull back and spit on his cock, guiding my hand up and down his shaft in a fast motion, twisting at the head, just as I saw him do to himself earlier.

Looking back up at him, Alex's mouth is open, cheeks flushed, and he seems to have caught his breath. I smirk and lean in, flicking my tongue over his bottom lip, catching it with my teeth and biting hard enough to break him out of his reverie. His eyes roll back and he bucks in my hand, his arms crushing me to him, hands roaming over my spine and cupping the back of my neck, bringing me into a searing kiss.

I keep kissing him through his orgasm, as he coats my hand and I swallow each and every one of his moans. Alex keeps holding me to him long after our breathing slows and our chests stop heaving, and I think to myself—*I want him forever.*

ELEVEN

I blink awake and stretch my arms, arching my spine. I feel...*amazing*. That was the best sleep I've gotten in the last few months and every single muscle in my body is relaxed. I moan and nuzzle deeper into the pillow, enjoying the warmth at my back.

Alex's arm wraps around me under the blanket, fingers toying with my nipple. I don't even think he's fully awake or aware that he's doing it. His lips find my shoulder and he leaves a small kiss there, and just that little act of intimacy makes my heart full. I wriggle some more, pulling him closer to me, feeling the hard ridge of his cock against my ass.

His hand tightens on my breast, fully cupping it and kneading. *Fuck, it feels so good.* How can I still want him so much when we already spent an amazing night together? Granted, we didn't actually have penetrative sex, so maybe I need to feel him inside me all the way in order to scratch this itch. Somehow, I doubt I'll have enough even then.

After we gave each other mind-blowing orgasms on the couch, we took a shower together. Alex's hands were in my hair, gently washing it and massaging my scalp, and I all but melted into him. We stayed under the spray of water until the droplets turned cold and we both started shivering. Even then, we only reluctantly broke apart from our languid kisses. It was like we didn't want to let each other go, didn't want to put an end to our blissful truce.

Truce.

That can't be all this is. From the moment I met him, I recognized the magnetic pull between us. If it wasn't for that day in the conference room where I heard him disrespecting me and my team, we might have been in this bed much, much sooner.

"Alex?" I say tentatively.

"Hmm," he responds, peppering my shoulder with more kisses, hand trailing lower down my stomach. I grab it and thread our fingers together, and he seems to break out of his sleepy haze.

"You okay?" he asks, voice gravely from sleep, lifting up on one elbow to look down at me.

I turn in his arms and face him, our hands still clasped together. He blinks down at my naked body revealed when the blanket pulls down, but he brings his gaze back to me. I don't miss the way his pupils expand with want, but I need to be sure before we take this further.

"I know we had a similar conversation last week, but—I want to make sure that this isn't just—" I say, huffing out a frustrated sigh.

"Just a hookup?" he asks, and I nod back at him.

"I want to make sure you still don't despise me or my team."

Alex huffs against my lips and drops a quick peck at the corner of my mouth. Pulling back, he gives me an incredulous look. "I am so sorry I ever made you feel that way," he says, eyes soft and looking more hazel in the morning light, mirroring my own. "I could never despise you. You drive me crazy sometimes, but I've liked you from the moment you walked into that café and gave me shit for stealing your drink."

I laugh and he joins in, reaching for my hands and bringing them over my head, fingers interlocked. The laugh dies in my throat as I feel him hard and hot against my core.

Alex sucks in a breath and pulls back a little so he doesn't fully crush me, but I'm still delectably pressed into the mattress, his weight on top of me. "You're witty and funny as hell. And whether you're practicing or hitting the gym, or fighting with me, you get this determined gleam in your eyes and—it's fucking thrilling to see, Malia."

My name on his lips is a throaty rasp and I lift up, stealing a kiss. He chases it, fingers tightening on mine, his cock rubbing on my thigh. "You drive me crazy Alex. But I like it—a lot."

Another kiss, this one longer and messier, showing each other how much this means, how much more it can be. Pulling back, he says, "I'm not an easy person to love, Malia. And I should tell you to run; I should tell you that being with me won't be easy, not just because of our jobs." I shake my head, but he keeps going, "But I want to try. Because I think we bring out the best in each other."

Smiling, I break free of his hold and throw my hands around his neck. "I've noticed that you haven't gotten into a single fight since I started coming to games. What's up with that, Cap?" I ask, teasing him.

Alex kisses me again, returning the smile against my lips. "I wanted you to come back. I quite like seeing you in that front row seat."

"Am I your good luck charm?"

His teeth scrape the sensitive skin at my neck before he

continues down my body, licking and teasing until I start to writhe under him.

"Should I wear you around my neck? I wouldn't mind being buried in your pussy again."

I gasp at his words but stop him before he can get lower. I don't think my clit can take anymore after last night. "You can wear my hand around your neck," I say sweetly, tilting his head up and feeling him swallow.

His grin is wild and bigger than any smile he's ever given me. "Don't tease me, baby."

Biting my lip, I push him until our positions are reversed and he's lying down, staring up at me with awe and so much lust. "You have no idea how many times I've wanted to wrap my hands around your throat and squeeze," I say, immediately blushing. Maybe I shouldn't have said that. What if he thinks it's weird?

But Alex doesn't kink shame me; if anything, he's even harder against me as my fingers twitch around his throat. He covers my hand with his and increases the pressure and my eyes widen, not once looking away from his gaze. "Take what you need. I want to see you come apart on my cock."

Searching his face, I say, "Are you sure?"

He grins and my heart soars again. Fuck, he may not be perfect, but he's damn near close.

"I'm on the pill, and clean," I say.

"I was tested a few months ago, so same here. Haven't been with anyone since."

"Really?" I ask, surprised.

"Yes, really," Alex growls and pulls me closer on top of him, the tip of his cock teasing my entrance.

I kiss him sweetly and add pressure to his throat. His nostrils flare once before he relaxes under me, and I use the opportunity to sink onto his cock. With how wet I am, I easily take him to the hilt.

"Fuck," he groans, head thrown back, looking like a fantasy come to life under me. Once I get used to the fullness of his cock inside me, I sit up more and start moving.

Alex brings one hand to my waist, guiding me on top, his hips snapping up to meet mine. We don't tease each other anymore. It's just the sound of slapping skin, moans, and grunts as we chase our orgasms. When he pulls me to him, kissing me wildly, my hand finds his throat again.

Not one to be upstaged, Alex reaches down and presses the pad of his thumb to my clit. We come together in a flurry of movement and harsh breaths, profanities flying from our lips. I shake on top of him and bite his shoulder as his hips stutter and he twitches inside me.

Later, when we finally get out of bed, he cleans me up, dresses me in his black sweatshirt and a pair of his sweatpants, and makes me breakfast. He keeps me in his sight at all times, like I might disappear if he blinks. He finds ways to touch me the entire time we eat, fingers threading through mine, caressing my shoulder, cupping the back of my head.

And even after, as we lazily sit on his couch and watch a holiday movie, my head rests in his lap, and his hand plays with my hair.

Alex says he's hard to love, but I get the feeling that it's the easiest thing I'll do.

TWELVE

Two Weeks Later

ALEX and I have been spending as much of our free time together as possible before my season starts, mostly hanging out at his apartment or going out on cozy dates.

We spent New Year's Eve together as I attended the Manticores game, and we went hand in hand to the after-party. The guy I have *feelings* for was there, holding my hand, dancing with me, and pressing me against the wall for a kiss at midnight. For the first time in a while, I stopped being so stressed out—and that is all because of Alex. These past few weeks, he's taken care of me in a way that no one else has—not since I lived with my family back home.

Alex is dependable and fiercely protective of the people he loves, and I can't even believe I ever despised him. Being with him is incredible and I don't regret it for a second. But my relationship with my coach has soured ever since he found out our fake dating turned into very real feelings.

Jackson has been constantly telling me I need to focus

and that I shouldn't be dating Alex. Ironic, when he was the one that pushed this idea so much and got marketing on his side to make it happen.

I've been taking it in stride, avoiding Jackson as much as I can, but being constantly berated and treated like a child is exhausting. He's been "improving" our gym routine, which basically means he's working us harder than ever and the whole team is already feeling burned out when the season hasn't even started.

But the worst part is the doubt that Jackson puts in my head. I've dreaded today's meeting with him ever since I saw the calendar invite. I know exactly why he's so pissed, but I take a deep inhale and walk into his office anyway.

"So you can disentangle yourself from your new boyfriend after all," he says in a biting tone.

"Jackson." I sigh and rub my temples, feeling a headache coming on already. "Not once have I been late to any practices or events you've set up for me. Why are you so hell-bent about this?"

"Because all of our asses are on the line here. You need to deliver the best fucking season of volleyball this arena has ever seen. Actual people are coming to these games, do you understand that? Do you understand that if you fail, this will all be over?"

I nod along, but he's just getting more and more worked up. "You need to focus. Fucking that slut hockey player of yours is taking your head out of the game," he tells me.

The worst part is that I've just come here after one of my most gruesome workouts. I know what's on the line. My legs are shaking and I can barely catch my breath, but what I hate most is the way he's talking about Alex.

"Don't you dare call him that again," I whisper furiously, balling my fists at my side.

He laughs at me and dismisses me with a flick of his hand. "Get out of my sight. If you don't break it off before the season opener, I'm going to find a way to do it for you," he threatens.

I can almost feel my blood boiling but I'm once again frozen and helpless, because there's nothing I can do. I have to just *take* it. His bullshit, his ire, *all of it*.

"I'll deal with it," I say, trying to appease him for now.

Except I won't be breaking anything off, because I care about Alex. He's the one person that brightens up my day.

When I get out of Jackson's office, I see the back of my boyfriend's head as he takes big steps towards the exit.

"Alex!" I yell, hoping he's here to take me to his place. Except he doesn't turn or listen to me. *Did he overhear me just now?*

I jog after him and my muscles scream in protest.

"Alex, wait."

He finally slows and I heave out a few breaths. "Al—"

"Are you *ever* going to stand up to him? Fight for what you want?" Alex turns to me, face red and green eyes blazing. I'm stunned to see that fury aimed at me, and even though my immediate response is to cry, I blink away the tears before they get a chance to form. He lets out a slow breath and looks ashamed of his reaction but keeps his distance.

"I'm sorry you overheard that, but it's not what you think," I choke out.

"So you weren't considering breaking up with me just to make your coach happy? After everything you've told me about him and how you owe him your career, you're telling me you were gonna fight for me?"

I take a step backwards, shoulders dropping in disappointment. "I wouldn't give you up so easily. And for the record, I was going to come talk to you about it and figure out our next steps as a *couple*."

Alex flinches at the word and I don't know if it's because he knows he messed up by blowing this out of proportion or because he doesn't like the concept of us being a couple, but I don't have the mental capacity to deal with it.

"Go home. I'll call you when I'm ready to talk," I say over my shoulder as I walk away.

MY APARTMENT IS cold and lonely when I get back and I miss Alex's sheets and the way he wraps me up in a blanket, making me into a Sherpa burrito because he knows I'm always chilly.

He's texted and called me at least a dozen times, leaving voicemails and apologizing for his reaction, and the truth is I've already forgiven him. Because if I were in his shoes, I would be pissed too after overhearing that conversation. But as much as I want to talk to him, I don't want either of us to say anything further that we'll regret.

Instead, I call my mom, and I cry my heart out, telling her all the ways Jackson has convinced me that the most important thing was work. I also tell her how much I miss her and my dad and brother. And because it feels good to finally get things off my chest, I also tell her about Alex.

"Did I make a mistake in asking for some space?"

"No, honey. I think it's important to step back when things get too heated. Besides, it sounds like you've been spending a lot of time together. Maybe a night away could do you both some good," Mom says in her sweet teacher voice.

"I guess." I sniff.

"You know what they say, absence makes the heart grow fonder and all that." She chuckles.

"I wish you guys could be here for the first game." I sigh wistfully.

"Us too, honey. We miss you so much," she says, a hint of sadness entering her voice.

"I'll call more, I promise," I say, before wishing her a good night.

After a long, hot shower and another good cry, I decide to call Alex. He answers on the second ring and for a second, I don't know what to say.

"Malia?"

"Hey," I say lamely.

"Sweetheart, I'm so sorry for the way I reacted. I was being an idiot and trying to push you away when I thought you might listen to Jackson," he says shakily. I can picture him sitting on his dark gray couch, dressed in nothing but his black sweatpants, a tattooed arm flexing with the movement of running his hand through his hair.

"And the truth is, I don't even blame you if you wanted to break things off, because, well—" He sighs, and it breaks my heart how defeated he sounds. "Because I'm not good at this whole relationship thing. You deserve better," he says, quietly enough that I barely hear it.

"Stop," I say, shaking my head even though he can't see me. "Alex, you *are* good at it. You're the best boyfriend I've ever had."

"The only boyfriend," he mumbles, and I chuckle.

"Okay, yes, technically the only official boyfriend I've ever had. But I mean it, you're thoughtful and kind and you take care of me. And most importantly, you challenge me. Look," I say, biting my lip, wanting to tell him that I'm falling for him and that I need him.

Instead, I say, "I forgive you for the outburst, but I want to make something clear." Taking a deep breath, I continue, "I really, really care about you and I'm not going to easily give up on us. Whether you like it or not." I add the last part jokingly, but Alex is quiet on the other end of the phone. I chew on my lip, worrying that I've said too much, too soon.

Say something, anything.

"Can I come see you?" he asks after a beat.

It's not what I expect him to say, and I hesitate. "It's pretty late, and I have practice in the morning. Not to mention you're about to go on a road trip."

"Exactly, I don't want to leave things off like this," he insists.

"Like what? I promise we're fine. Trust me. We'll call and text while you're gone this week. And then Friday when you get back, I want you to come to my season opener. I *need* you there."

"Okay." He breathes out, giving in to my request. "Of course I'll be there. I won't miss it for the world."

THIRTEEN

The winter weather advisory message on my phone mocks me as I enter the arena. It's the day before our most important game of the season, and things are already going to shit.

Our adversaries, a relatively new team from Buffalo, are having issues with their travel arrangements to come to Grand Marquee. Tomorrow's game has officially been postponed by two hours, and we're hoping that's the best-case scenario.

The news is calling it one of our whitest storms of the year, blowing in from the East, causing whiteouts and accidents from Boston all the way to Buffalo and heading towards Michigan and the rest of the Midwest.

My phone rings and I quickly take it out of my jacket, sliding to answer.

"Alex? Is everything okay?"

"Hey," he says quickly, and I can barely hear him over the background noise. Alex's away games were on the East coast this week and he's supposed to play in Massachusetts tonight before taking the bus back to Grand Marquee. "I have some bad news," he says, and my shoulders drop.

"You won't make it by tomorrow night?" I ask miserably.

"I'm going to do everything in my power to get there, but—" He stops himself, the growing chatter behind him getting louder and louder.

"But what?"

He must step out because all of a sudden it's quiet except for the sounds of his breathing. "Our game tonight got canceled, which means we're headed back to Grand Marquee earlier than expected."

"That's good, right?" I say, hope overtaking me. I'll finally see him again.

"Yes and no. I tried getting a flight, but everything was canceled or delayed and I'd rather not risk it. The bus should get us there in time *if* there are no issues on the roads, but it looks bad out there, at least in a few of the states we have to pass through."

"Oh," I say dejectedly. I can't even muster up a lie to tell him I'm fine, because I'm not. My first game of my professional career, and no one I know will be here for me.

Alex must pick up on my sadness because he says, "I'm going to do my best to make it. I promise."

"Yeah, I know. Thank you," I say, choking a little on my tears. Until I see Jackson heading for me. Then I try to compose myself.

"Malia, I lo—"

"Alex, I gotta go, I'll talk to you later," I say, and hang up right as Jackson stops in front of me.

"Ready for tomorrow night?" he asks.

"Respectfully, Coach," I say, wiping my tears off with my sleeve, "I think we need to take it easy today. The last thing we need is to be burned out tomorrow."

He squints at me, narrowing his eyes. "Oh god, why are

you crying? You know I can't deal with tears. Did you break things off with your boyfriend yet?"

"That's an inappropriate question and none of your business, *Coach*." I would be much prouder of myself for standing up to him if it wasn't for the massive hole in my chest that misses Alex, that misses my family. God, how I wish they could be here so I can show them that I'm done taking this man's bullshit.

Jackson looks uncomfortable, and I think my little act of defiance has taken him by surprise. He huffs, but lets me run the practice at a slower pace, and all the girls are excited about what's to come.

"Cap, we're throwing an after-party tomorrow night at The Arcadian. I think we should all celebrate, no matter the outcome of the game," Jonie says.

"First off," I say, palm out in front of her, "I think you mean we'll celebrate our *win* tomorrow, because we are going to crush Buffalo."

My teammates whoop and cheer and it makes me smile. Maybe I don't need anyone here tomorrow, because I have them—my two best friends, and my team. They'll be sharing this special night with me.

"Second off," I say when they've quieted down, "I want you to know I'm really proud of you all. You've all worked so incredibly hard these past few months training, practicing, really becoming a cohesive team. I couldn't imagine doing this with any other group of talented ladies."

"Right back at you, Cap," Andrea says, wiping a tear off her cheek.

"So yes, tomorrow we'll celebrate our season opener, today we'll get some rest so we can play our best. Go home, I'll see you all tomorrow."

THE ARENA IS ONLY HALF full when warmups start half an hour before the game, which is a little disheartening. We run through a series of passing, blocking, and pepper drills as people start to filter in, taking their seats courtside and in the lower sections of the arena.

I don't have my phone on me, otherwise I would check Alex's location for the millionth time. Their bus broke down somewhere in Pennsylvania and he decided to rent a car and drive back with some of his friends. I'm more nervous than ever, because what if something happens to him and it's all my fault? I told him I needed him to be here and all but hung up on him while he was trying to tell me something important yesterday.

We haven't gotten the chance to properly catch up and talk about the words he almost said to me before Jackson interrupted our call, just quick messages here and there, sharing his location with me so I'd stop worrying.

My eyes roam over every seat anyway, like I might be able to conjure him out of thin air.

"Malia!" an excited voice pulls my attention.

"Josh!" I say and run up to him, giving him a hug. Jen is nearby, keeping an eye on him. Turns out that Michael needed someone to babysit Josh and he called none other than Jen, our talented team photographer. I nod at her and she gives me a small smile.

"I have a surprise for you," he says, turning around and showing off the back of his T-shirt with my name and number on it.

"Aw, I'm honored, kid," I say, tearing up.

"It was actually Uncle Alex's idea. He got us all T-shirts."

"What do you mean?" I ask and Josh's eyes go wide.

"Oh shit, I wasn't supposed to say that," he whispers.

"Not supposed to say what?"

"Hey Cap, we need to go get ready," Andrea says with an apologetic smile.

"Okay, yeah," I say, nodding. "I'll see you later, kid. I really appreciate you being here," I say and give him another tight hug.

After twenty minutes of getting ready in the locker room, we are pumped and set to start the season off with a bang. Jackson gives us what I'm sure he considers a great speech. But the girls all look to me for a final word of encouragement and that feels like a monumental step. I want to be a good leader and more than anything, I want them to trust me.

Once the girls start lining up in the hallway to be introduced for their entrance, I take a moment to myself in the locker room, letting the anticipation fuel me. I don't see any messages on my phone, but I snap a picture of my locker, where my name plate is right under Alex's, and send it to him.

The locker room door creaks open and I yell out, "I'll be right there!"

I bite my lip and start to type out a text to Alex.

> Look how far we've come. I can't wait to tell you in person how much I I—

A large hand takes the phone from my hand. I'm so stunned that I spin around, ready to yell at Jackson, except —a familiar woodsy smell envelops me and when I look up, I'm met with the most gorgeous green eyes.

"You don't get to say it first."

I take a stuttering breath, but I don't get to reply because Alex picks me up and kisses me hard, lips cold and bruising against mine as my legs easily wrap around his waist.

He holds me there, both panting, our foreheads touching, until I hear that they've started announcing the players.

I sigh and press another kiss to his mouth. "I have to go."

He nods and sets me down, his hands finding mine and lifting them to his lips, pressing another cold kiss to my knuckles. "I can't wait to watch you kick ass."

"I missed you so much," I say, dragging him with me to the door as I get in line.

Alex stops me once more with a tug on my hand. "Try not to get distracted by the people in my section, okay?"

I narrow my eyes, wondering what he means by that. Alex kisses me again, a soft peck on the lips, and sprints out through another hallway.

I'm left there, waiting for my name to be called, my lips tingling, my heart full, and ready to play the best game of my life.

"Ladies and gentlemen, please welcome to the court the Thunderbirds' captain, Malia Kahale!" the announcer says in an excited voice, and the—now almost full to the brim—arena erupts into cheers.

One section is louder than all the others and I look behind me at the large group of people cheering me on with signs and shirts with "Kahale" and the number "6" on them.

And among those people, my parents and my brother, with tears in their eyes, clapping the hardest. My legs almost give out and I can't stop the blinding smile that overtakes my face.

They're here.

How are they here?

It all clicks as my dad throws an arm around Alex's shoulder, the image almost comical as my dad is five inches shorter.

Alex did this. He flew my parents in. *For me.*

I give them all a wave and mouth "Thank you" to Alex. Not only did he bring my family, but he brought his too. Michael and Josh are there, and so are Robbie, Jordan, and Trip.

And my heart is full. Full of love for this man and everything that he is.

"I love you," he mouths to me right before everyone stands for the national anthem. I shake my head at him.

He *really* didn't want me to say it first.

THE LOCKER ROOM is buzzing after our 3-2 win over Buffalo. After we all shower, we head over to The Arcadian, where the after-party is taking place. I'm congratulated by a sea of strangers, but the only people I care about are sitting together at a large table, sharing food and stories about me.

"Do you remember the one time she broke her foot playing volleyball on the beach?" my mom asks my dad, about to tell an embarrassing story that I probably don't even remember.

"Guys, I can't believe you're here," I interrupt, giving them all hugs and trying my best not to cry big fat tears of joy.

Alex waits his turn patiently, and I love him all the more for it. Always thoughtful, always considerate. He comes back from the bar with a cocktail for me, but I only take a small sip of the peanut butter and whiskey concoction before setting it down and dragging him outside through the back door.

He chuckles. "What are you doing? It's freezing out here."

I walk him back against the brick wall of the alley and he lets me lead, a curious spark in his eyes. "Say it out loud this time," I beg.

That spark becomes a full-fledged fire as he cups my face, bringing me on my tiptoes for a sweet, languid kiss. When he finally pulls back from my lips, he says, "I love you so much."

I can't stop smiling.

I can't stop kissing him, can't stop dragging my hands

across his chest, fisting the athletic shirt with my name on it, wanting so badly to see him wear it at *every* game this season. And for once, that wanting is not so far-fetched. Because he loves me and he'll be there for me, time and time again.

I know it in my bones. Alex is the only person for me. My loving, adoring, sometimes-a-pain-in-my-ass *soulmate*.

"I love you too."

EPILOGUE

One Year Later
Alex

THE ARENA IS SOLD out for the first time this season and the pressure to win this game is higher than ever. I can't believe it: my *last* game with the Manticores.

I always thought I would be a part of this team until the end of my career. Not that I would be traded at twenty-seven. I've dedicated my last eight years to Grand Marquee, and it feels bittersweet to say goodbye, especially when we did so well last year, bringing home the Calder Cup.

But it wouldn't have been nearly as satisfying if I didn't have *her* by my side.

Malia. The love of my life and future wife.

I would have married her on the spot that night a year ago when she told me she loved me back. I would have dragged her sassy ass to City Hall the next day if it was up to me, but she wanted me to be sure, to pace myself. So I did.

I wanted to prove to her that I was the man she deserved. Some days I still don't feel like I am, but she always seems to know how to squash those bad thoughts.

The ring I bought has been hiding in my shaving kit for the last month, knowing that's the last place she'd ever look through at my apartment. *Our* apartment now, since she moved in over the summer.

I was going to propose over Christmas while we took the world's shortest trip to Hawaii to visit her family, but while we were there, she got a call from a volleyball team in Quebec, one that she's had her eye on after Jonie and Andrea got traded at the end of last season.

Malia is one of the best volleyball players I've ever seen, and I'm not just saying that because I love her. She's got so much talent that was being wasted with the Thunderbirds. Even though her teammates are decent, she could be so much better in the right environment and out from under Jackson's thumb.

So when the opportunity came for her to be traded to Quebec, I encouraged her to take it. We discussed options for long distance, but in the end, I knew I would follow her anywhere. So I requested a trade.

And while Malia is out there, setting up our new apartment, I'm ready to play my last game with the Manticores. Then I can join her and my new team, the Quebec Loonies.

AS THE GUYS filter into the locker room, I try to memorize this feeling. This place has been my home, my second family, for the longest time. And I'm going to miss it —*them*—like crazy. But I'll be back someday.

"Listen up, team," I say, standing up in half my gear, resting my hands on my hips. The room quiets and everyone turns their expectant gazes on me. "There's something I need to tell you all, and it's not easy."

I take a deep breath and find the eyes of my two closest friends, Robbie and Jordan. With a smile, I say, "About a month ago, I requested a trade to Quebec."

The room is still, and you could probably hear a pin drop right about now. Then it explodes into chaos, and I need to raise my voice to quiet everyone down. "One at a time, please."

"Why?" Jordan asks.

"Because the woman I want to marry is taking a new opportunity, and I want to be there for her."

"What about you?" Trip asks, a confused look on his face.

"What about me?" I ask, eyebrows raised.

He takes a moment to think his question through and lands on, "Well, don't you love it here? This team? Why couldn't you wait until the season was over, at least?"

I swallow and nod. "I've thought about it. I don't want you guys to think I'm abandoning you, because that's not what this is. The truth is, I haven't always loved the reputation that I got by playing for the Manticores. I've considered a fresh start more than once, and this was the perfect time to do it."

"Who's going to replace you?" one of the rookies asks.

"Thank you for asking, I was just about to get to that," I say, smiling and walking to my locker, pulling out a brand-new jersey.

I hope he'll like it, even though I'm blindsiding him with this.

I hold it out, the C for captain embroidered in black on the front of the jersey, his name staring up at me as I walk towards him. Stopping a foot away, I hold out a hand.

He stares at me, blue eyes wide and shining. Robbie clasps his hand in mine and I pull him up into a hug. "I couldn't think of anyone better equipped for the job."

His dark blond hair flops with the shake of his head as he grins at me. "I don't know what to say. Just—I won't let you down."

I nod and step back to address the room. "After tonight, Robbie's gonna be your new captain. Make sure you give him as much hell as you gave me," I say jokingly.

Everyone cheers and congratulates us both for our new opportunities and Robbie hangs his new jersey up, last name Elliot proudly displaying above number 31.

ACKNOWLEDGEMENTS

Thank you to Jen, Megan, Hilary, Debbie, and Leanne! This novella would not be what it is without your amazing feedback. You've helped me transform Alex from a Class A asshole to a lovable and thoughtful MMC.

Thank you to Lorissa for another incredible cover and to Erin for copy editing!

If you've read The Love Penalty and Bar Down and wanted more Manticores shenanigans, thank you for being here! There's one more book in this series—Delay of Game—which will be released Summer 2025.

You'll get Alice and Jordan's story, which many of you have been waiting for! But this novella had to be released first in order for you to meet these characters as Alex and Malia will make a few appearances in Delay of Game!

I hope you've enjoyed, and I can't wait for this series to be complete! See you soon.

ABOUT THE AUTHOR

Project leader by day, romance author by night, Stef C.R. lives in West Michigan with her husband and not one, not two, but three cats. When she's not working or writing stories, she spends her time reading fantasy and romance, endlessly cheering on the Red Wings, Charles LeClerc, and listening to Noah Kahan.

ARE you looking for romances with happily ever afters? Then let's escape into the world of swoony MMCs and unforgettable heroines together. Find more information at stefwritesstories.com!

www.ingramcontent.com/pod-product-compliance
Lightning Source LLC
LaVergne TN
LVHW012024060526
838201LV00061B/4444